JAWBONE LAKE

Also by Ray Robinson

Electricity
The Man Without
Forgetting Zoë

Ray Robinson

JAWBONE LAKE

WILLIAM HEINEMANN: LONDON

Published by William Heinemann 2014

2 4 6 8 10 9 7 5 3 1

First published in Great Britain in 2014 by
William Heinemann
Random House, 20 Vauxhall Bridge Road,
London SW1V 2SA

www.randomhouse.co.uk

Addresses for companies within The Random House Group Limited can be found at:
www.randomhouse.co.uk/offices.htm

The Random House Group Limited Reg. No. 954009

A CIP catalogue record for this book
is available from the British Library

ISBN 9780434022038

The Random House Group Limited supports the Forest Stewardship Council®
(FSC®), the leading international forest-certification organisation. Our books
carrying the FSC label are printed on FSC®-certified paper. FSC is the only forest-
certification scheme supported by the leading environmental organisations, including
Greenpeace. Our paper procurement policy can be found at
www.randomhouse.co.uk/environment

MIX
Paper from
responsible sources
FSC
www.fsc.org FSC® C016897

Typeset in Joanna MT Std by Palimpsest Book Production Limited,
Falkirk, Stirlingshire

Printed and bound in Great Britain by
Clays Ltd, St Ives plc

For
ADRIAN BRISCOE

New Year's Eve

STAVING OFF the chill, Rabbit tied the ear flaps of her trapper hat below her chin and blew warmth into her mittens. She strolled along the bay, just below the isolate, Slow Mile Bridge, spanning the northern tip of the lake. The full moon was so large, the stars so bright that night, that the lake ice appeared to be glowing, the snowy ground effervescent.

Sensing the vastness of the water out there, its pull, she was reminded how, towards the end of her labour last year, it felt as if her stomach had created its own field of gravity, within which everything in her life began to orbit. And even though he was now gone from her world, she still felt him inside her, floating like a tiny underwater astronaut.

When he came home from the hospital, she didn't really notice his sobbing, grizzling or wailing. She had a touch of the baby blues. Her Aunt Cass would change and feed him while Rabbit buried her head beneath a pillow, filled with a strange sorrow. But then she began to worry that he was becoming too familiar with Cass's smell, confusing their skin. Gradually, the shadowy strain of Rabbit's woe began to fade, and he would turn his head whenever she spoke or came into a room, lift his arms and cry out for her. Cass became but a mere satellite orbiting them both.

Arms like sausage meat, ears like fine shells, the tyres of flesh rolling from his neck down to his ankles – she could gobble him up, he was so gorgeous.

She missed him every day.

Rabbit paced the snowy shoreline, feeling the cold penetrate through her clothes. She was considering heading home when she heard what she thought were fireworks in the opposite valley, a sound in the sky like a water pipe stuttering. A light flickered by the bridge, moving the moon-shadows of the trees. She stopped, hugged herself.

Then she heard the skid of tyres and a flare of light cut an abrupt wedge through the darkness.

A vehicle careered across the bridge and smashed through the wall, engine whirring as its tyres lost purchase. It lurched through the air, nose-diving towards the ice until the moment of brutal impact. That sound, like the fabric of life tearing in two. A seam in the world coming undone.

The hungry suck of the lake. The vehicle tilted, rapidly disappearing beneath the surface, bubbles and debris breaching the hole in the ice.

Then she heard the whirr of another engine. Red tail lights reversing off the bridge, coming to a stop by the broken wall. A figure appeared, pointing towards the lake. A dark shape silhouetted in his hand.

She started to edge away but tripped in the snow. When she looked back, he was staring. He began to move.

Rabbit rushed into the tall pine trees, the flush of adrenalin making her light-headed, stumbling deeper into the woods. She didn't look back, but could sense him behind her. Stepping into her footprints, his eyes a hard glitter.

New Year's Day

Joe was awoken by the sound of his phone vibrating on the tabletop. He reached over. 6 a.m. It was his mother.

'You need to come home, son.'

'Why? What's wrong?'

He climbed out of bed and walked over to the window.

'Mum?'

'It's your dad . . .' She paused. 'There's been an accident. At the lake . . .'

Voices in the background. A muffled sob.

'He went off the bridge, Joe. Into the water. They say they've found the car –' her voice broke – 'but he's not . . . he's . . .'

'Mum, wait. Slow down. Start again.'

More voices now: soft, reassuring. 'Just get here,' she said. There was a click. The line went dead.

He called back – engaged. Again – still engaged. He dialled CJ's number. Straight to answerphone.

He stood by the window, staring past his own reflection at the neon smudge of London outside, and a sick feeling descended over him. He felt as if he was floating, free of time and space. He started throwing clothes into a bag, trying to picture Jawbone Lake in his mind, but the images turned back on themselves.

He left the motorway and took the B-roads into the snow-covered valleys, glimpsing the moon through the pine trees. The occasional flake fell into the beam of his headlights, now dim in the freezing dawn fog. He kept checking his phone. Nothing. He felt a sudden chill in the car and turned the heat up a couple of degrees. He travelled through the empty streets of Whatstandwell, Cromford and Matlock Bath, speeding towards a destination he wasn't sure he wanted to meet. Streets as quiet as the snow settling on the pavements.

Driving past a picnic spot, childhood memories washed over him, and he thought about the times when they were a tight unit – father and son – on camping trips, walking in inclement weather, Joe's legs barely long enough to keep up.

The valley got narrower above him, crags rising into the charcoal-grey sky as dawn approached over the easterly peaks.

At the southern end of Ravenstor, he took a right and followed the lake road up through Musdale. Around the final bend to Slow Mile Bridge – with the lakeshore through the pines to his left – he was brought to a standstill by a roadblock.

He stepped out of the car. A yellow Sea King helicopter thumped the air above him. He thought he was going to retch. He walked over to the police cordon. The attending officer wouldn't let him through.

'But have you found him?' Joe asked.

The officer opened his mouth, paused, and then shook his head. 'Sorry.'

He turned the car round and drove up the hillside, pulling over at a spot where townsfolk were huddled. A large area of ice had been hacked away beneath the bridge and around Horseshoe Bay, frogmen moving through the water. Winches, chainsaws, ice-diving gear and lifting bags. Brightly coloured buoys bobbing in the water, marking the spot.

His thoughts flicked back to the week before Christmas, the last time he saw him . . .

CJ had just flown in from Gibraltar. Father and son met at the Tube, and hugged briefly – a brisk, manly embrace, clapping each other on the back.

Back at the apartment, Joe had ordered a takeaway and listened to CJ in the shower singing 'Marlowe's Theme'.

He poured two fingers of whiskey into a glass.

The bathroom door opened and CJ appeared, shoulder-length hair dripping onto the towel around his shoulders, mobile to his ear. He winked at Joe.

He was a handsome devil. Women looked at him when he walked down the street. He would always smile back, a swagger to his step. At fifty-nine he was paunch-free, and, unlike Joe, had all his hair, though it was obvious he dyed it. Quick-witted and super-sharp, he was always two steps ahead of the conversation and could twist anything into a double entendre. He had the common touch. Everybody loved him.

'Christmas again, eh. So when are you coming up?'

Joe grimaced. 'I'm not coming this year. I'm . . . too busy.'

CJ's brown eyes focused in on his.

'Why? Is something up at work?'

'No, the company's fine. Doing really well, actually.' He paused. 'I've decided to sell it. We've had a few meetings, there's plenty of interest – but lots of loose ends to tie up.'

Joe had set up the software company as soon as he left university. Despite the occasional fright, it had thrived. CJ was a silent partner, but always checking in, and quick to voice his opinions.

Joe felt the atmosphere in the kitchen change. He rarely saw CJ angry, even as a kid, though he certainly had his moods – moods that had gravity, a presence – but he now looked genuinely displeased.

'All I know is the job's making me miserable,' Joe said. 'I'm so bored. I feel as useless as an appendix. I want to do something different for a while.'

CJ snorted. 'I see. So what do you want to be when you grow up?'

'Look, I built the business up from scratch.'

'I know, I was the one that helped you set it up, remember.'

'Well, I don't feel like I've had a break since I was twenty-one. I work every day. I can't remember the last time I had a holiday. I'm constantly scared I'll lose a contract. It's no life. I thought you'd understand.'

'You're giving up.'

'No, I've succeeded, and now I need to do something different. It's the right time to sell and you know it.'

12

The potential buyers, he explained, were larger software firms, or hardware companies, looking to expand their portfolio. 'And anyway,' he said, 'if it all goes tits up, I can always go back to it, can't I? But I've had enough. And enough of London. I'm renting this place out for a year. Maybe longer.'

CJ held his gaze a moment, shrugged, and walked back to the bedroom.

The takeaway arrived. CJ returned to his usual self. No mention of the company.

Sitting in the lounge together, plastic containers strewn across the coffee table between them, CJ lit a cigar. It was one of the smells of those long-ago evenings of Joe's childhood. Joe used to love sitting on CJ's lap before bedtime. Jumping onto him where he sat by the fire, a glass of whiskey in one hand, cigar in the other. He particularly liked it when CJ hadn't shaved, the sting of his bristles making him squeal. At that moment, Joe wanted to lean over and touch the stubble on his father's face.

CJ blew a smoke ring which hovered above his head. He appeared lost in thought. Present, but not really there.

'So what time are you off?' Joe asked.

'Taking the early train.' CJ flicked fat ash into a silver dish. 'Booked a cab at some unearthly hour. Probably gone before you're up.'

'I'll say my goodbyes now then, just in case,' Joe said. 'I'm off to bed.'

His father rose, and held out his arms. They hugged.

'Take care,' Joe said. 'And send my love to Mum.'

'Will do.'

Joe nodded at the whiskey. 'And don't sit up drinking all night.'

Goodbye.

He parked beside a patrol car on the ploughed driveway, climbed from his Audi, and peered up at the large stone house, checking the mullioned windows for movement inside. He stepped into the hall and the familiar smell of his childhood home – oak floors, panelled walls, damp boots in the cloak cupboard – took him by the throat. He could hear voices coming from the direction of the living room.

His mother, Eileen, was holding a mug of tea, and Bill, his grandfather, sat beside her on the couch, poised, as if waiting for her to collapse.

'Mum.'

She glanced at him briefly, nodded, and then stared down into her mug, tired and red around the eyes. He wanted to go over and embrace her but felt rooted to the spot.

She'd aged since he'd last seen her; there was a sagging at the corners of her mouth, small pouches of world-weariness, dissatisfaction. But she was still pretty.

Despite smoking a packet of Menthols a day, she did fifty lengths at the local swimming pool twice a week and refused to go the way of most of her post-menopausal friends and chop off her hair. She loved to shop and to dress up, though she could never be called mutton. A woman who would slap your hand if you swore in front of her. She had a part-time job, the same job she'd had since she finished technical college at eighteen, working as the administrator for a firm that specialised in industrial engineering, plumbing and DIY supplies in the neighbouring valley.

'Mum,' he repeated.

Bill nodded at him, as if to say everything was going to be OK. Joe noticed the fine red delta on his grandfather's cheeks, the tonsure of silver hair sticking up, and his bony, never-idle hands flapping about. His pyjamas were poking out of his trouser bottoms and he didn't have any socks on.

Joe saw his father in Bill's troubled face, and an echo of the nausea he felt beside Slow Mile Bridge returned.

The local church minister walked into the room with a plate of biscuits, placed them on the coffee table and sank back in an armchair, a prayer book resting on its arm. Eileen fixed him with a cold stare.

'Can you leave, please?' Her voice had a hard tone to it. 'I know you mean well, but I don't want you here.'

Red-faced, the minister silently nodded, and left the room. Joe could hear murmuring at the front door, and the sound of shoes being wiped. He craned his head – a man in a tight grey suit entered, grasping a notebook and pen.

Eileen looked towards Joe, and in a businesslike manner, she said, 'This is DI Slater. He's in charge of the investigation.'

Joe nodded at the man.

'Mr Slater, this is Joe. Our boy.'

The man reached for Joe's hand and shook it firmly. Side-parted, his dark hair had an incredible sheen to it and his suit had a single button at the front which looked like it would pop if he flexed his pecs too sharply. He sat down in the recently vacated armchair.

'I'm sorry to have kept you waiting,' he said. 'We're still setting up at the crash site.'

'So what can you tell us?' Joe said. 'They wouldn't let me near. Was he drunk? Was he speeding?'

Slater made a steeple with his hands, opening his mouth to speak.

Joe interrupted. 'Had he swerved to avoid a sheep or deer or something? Could he have swum to safety? Maybe he had a stroke or heart attack. Maybe he fell asleep at the wheel or hit some ice. I mean, what's happening down there?'

'All good questions,' Slater said. 'And I wish I had the answers for you. The CIU, the Collision Investigation Unit, they're examining the scene now. We've had specialist units brought in. The Fire and Rescue Service have provided thermal imaging equipment, and an underwater search team experienced in these sorts of conditions is down there as we speak.'

This way of talking. The antiseptic police nomenclature and use of acronym – Joe found it comforting, reassuring.

'What will the Collision Unit be looking for?' Joe asked, and Eileen raised her eyes to look at him.

'Hard evidence. Marks on the road. Trying to establish if there was a mechanical fault with the vehicle. Speed upon impact. Paint marks on the stonework. Essentially we'll be trying to piece together the sequence of events that led to CJ's vehicle leaving the road.'

Joe heard a noise in the room, an almost imperceptible rattling sound. He slid a glance at Bill who was still gazing at Eileen.

'Where's the car now?' Joe asked.

'It will have to be dried off in a sterile environment before the forensic team can examine it. The crime scene investigators will continue with their inquiries under the management of the forensic scientists. The first officers on the scene arrived just after 3 a.m. There was a lot of debris in the hole in the ice, which had already started to freeze over. A torch. Blanket. Walking boots. Items Eileen identified earlier.'

Eileen looked at Joe, blinking rapidly, as if to erase the memory.

'The vehicle was around six metres down,' Slater continued. 'We had to get heavy equipment to the scene to help remove it from the ice. There was no sign of Mr Arms.'

Joe realised where the unusual sound was coming from; it was the flutter of Eileen's jaw. Her teeth were chattering.

'But could he have got out?' Joe asked.

'It's possible. The windscreen was missing.' He paused. 'And both of the front windows were down.'

'Down? Both of them?'

Eileen laughed, a dry cough of a laugh. She put the mug of tea on the floor and placed her face in her hands. Bill rubbed her back in circles.

'And the dive team?' Joe asked. 'How long will they be there for?'

'It's difficult to say. The search parameters will change daily.'

Bill chipped in. 'Is there any news on the caller?'

'What caller?' Joe asked.

Slater nodded slowly, a solemn look on his face. 'An anonymous call was made from the phone box on the edge of Nether Tor estate. A woman. To say she'd witnessed the crash.'

'Why would she phone the police and not give her name?'

'We're following a few lines of inquiry.'

'But why would someone do that?'

'We're checking CCTV footage from around the area this morning, but there are no cameras on that side of Nether Tor.'

'Why don't you just release the recording, play it on local TV or radio?'

'Enough, Joe,' Eileen snapped. 'Please.'

Joe sat on his bed and took a hard look at his old room. It felt hollow, detached. He went over to the window and watched snow fleck the valley. In the distance, the white peak of High Tor looked vivid in the fading light. Snow lay heavy across the rectangles of higgledy-piggledy rooftops descending into the valley below. Cars progressed beneath the orange stars of street lights, familiar constellations snaking between the mass of hill, tor, fell. Life, going on as normal.

He cast a glance at his bag. He couldn't bring himself to unpack.

The house was quiet. Earlier, Bill had raised his voice at one of the police officers. Soon after, the officer drove Bill home so that he could get dressed properly and collect a few things. He was now in the spare bedroom, across the landing, noisily moving things around.

Joe pictured Eileen downstairs in the living room, sitting on the couch, staring into space. He'd offered to make her something to eat but she whispered she wanted to be on her own.

None of them appeared to know what to do. Grieving on hold, waiting for the news that no one wanted to come.

Joe eyed the northerly peaks through his window. CJ loved being out there, exploring remote villages and pubs. Monsal Head. Water-cum-Jolly. His favourite place was Gibbet Rock in Cressbrook Dale. It reminded him of St Peter's in Rome.

Joe leaned his forehead against the cold glass. Watched tears drop from his nose onto the back of his hand.

There was a knock at the door. Eileen's head appeared. 'I'm going out of my mind just sitting here. I need to look.'

To avoid been seen by the police, press or any of the locals rubbernecking near Slow Mile Bridge, they took the old drovers' track that led to the middle of the lake.

The full moon and swatch of stars lit the surrounding bowl of hills in an insipid, blue-white light, picking out scalloped ice in boot-shaped puddles. Snow fell in a half-arsed way, flakes suspended as if by pieces of thread. Ahead of them, rowing boats sat frozen into the ice beside a jetty, and, in the far distance, police searchlights illuminated the crash site. The dive teams were still out there, down there, beneath the water and ice. Joe imagined them moving through water, their oily black suits like whale skin, and the enormity of the search struck him for the very first time. Such a vast, deep lake.

Bill moved away from them both to stand on his own, a dark figure looking out, searching for movement, a shape. The temperature was nudging ten below zero and Joe felt the cold in his body meat.

Eileen shouted into the darkness, 'CJ!'

A dog responded distantly, followed by the crack and boom of the ice sheet, the hills throwing the sounds around. In their slow wake, silence.

Joe used to come here torchlight fishing with CJ. The dark early mornings felt like hell but he loved being out on the lake, drilling holes through the ice, portals into the underwater world, drinking coffee from a flask as CJ attempted to steep him in the lore of the Peaks. Stories about the hills and tors CJ had climbed, about the days he'd spent wandering the countryside, about the village below their feet. The valley was flooded in the 1920s to provide water for the Peak District. Twenty-three houses, a church, school, five farms and some 1,100 acres of land were submerged under the lake. The resulting reservoir, when viewed from the hills, bore a clear resemblance to a jawbone. They felt naming the reservoir after the drowned Coldwater village would be a bad omen.

And as the cold hours slipped by, waiting for the tipping of the rod, Joe liked to imagine the clutch of streets below, the submerged houses beneath the lake.

Joe stood in the moonlight, picturing CJ struggling against the water, against his clothes that may as well have been a suit of armour. The family belonged to the world above, CJ below, the ice a barrier between the two.

Eileen called out again. 'CJ. CJ!'

Joe wanted to go out there. He wanted to smash a hole through the ice with his fists.

RABBIT LAY in bed listening to Cass moving about downstairs. Her heart was beating too fast. The more she thought about it, the faster it got.

Thumps on the stairs. Cass appeared behind the door.

'Happy new year, sleepyhead.'

Rabbit sat up.

'You've not heard the news.'

'What news?'

'A crash. Slow Mile Bridge.'

Rabbit stared.

'All the roads are closed. Police everywhere. It's all they're talking about on the radio. You all right?'

'Uh-huh.'

'Wrap up,' Cass said. 'Let's go see.'

Rabbit shook her head. 'No. Actually, I don't feel too good. You go.'

Cass tutted. 'Hung-over, more like.'

Cass was gone for over an hour. When she came back, Rabbit hadn't moved.

'There's a big crowd,' Cass said, visibly excited. 'We had

to stand on the edge of Musdale. The whole bridge is cordoned off. There's this marquee thing down on the bay, and men in white boiler suits, and a whole load of police and sniffer dogs standing around. It's like something from *Prime Suspect*.'

'Do they know who it is?'

'Yes. But they can't find him.'

'Who?'

'It's CJ Arms.'

Rabbit knew the man's name, but she wasn't sure she'd ever met him.

Cass looked at her gravely. 'You all right?'

'Yes. Fine. Just a bit tired, that's all. It was a big night.'

A dream: she is stumbling through the pine woods, through snow that comes up to her waist. Short bursts of breath in the moonlight, like dirty liquid. Her lungs burn, thighs ache. When she stops and holds her breath to listen, she can hear him approaching.

She blinked up at the ceiling; she could see the impressions of her feet in the snow.

Rabbit sat up in bed. The light had almost faded. The evening was freezing cold. She walked to the open window and drew the curtains back a little. The outwoods, a dark shape on the perimeters of the estate, looked threatening as the trees waved in a breeze, making their shadows dance in the empty streets.

No one there.

She got back into bed and pictured the marquee down

on Horseshoe Bay. She imagined CJ's body inside. Those beating hearts surrounding that non-beating corpse. A police photographer taking shots of the body, bloated and white like some grotesque fish.

Exposed in the flashgun.

CIGARETTE SMOKE escaped from the window of the silver Mercedes, wraithlike. Grogan watched the estate. Drumming his fingers on the steering wheel, he closed his eyes to recall her better. Five feet five inches tall. Chequered trapper hat. Green or bluish coat with a furry hood. Wisps of blonde hair. But her face remained a blank disc.

No matter how long it took, he had to find her. Make her disappear.

Across White Peak, the sun went down on New Year's Day. The valley held the darkness like a coffin.

Week One

THOSE FIRST few days of sleeplessness and clock-watching. CJ's shadow stalked the house; he was in the kitchen in the morning making coffee and toast; he sang theme songs in the shower and sat in his chair beside the fireplace, puffing on a cigar.

Bill had gone into cleaning mode while Eileen ran herself one bath after another, sobbing into the bubbles, or she dozed on the couch, refusing to go upstairs to the conjugal bed. She could smell CJ in the sheets, she said. The three of them headed back and forth to Jawbone, leaving the house by the back twitchel, hoods pulled up against the world, searching, listening to the ice.

He woke to voices out on the landing and opened his bedroom door to find two police officers walking down the stairs, one of them carrying CJ's computer, the other a box of lever arch files.

Eileen was standing in the doorway to CJ's study.

'What's going on?' Joe asked.

'What does it look like?' She followed the police officers down the stairs.

The toilet flushed along the landing and Bill appeared, wiping his hands on his shirt.

'They said it's just routine, youth.'

'Right.'

'But I think they reckon otherwise. There are no such things as accidents, Joe.'

'What does that mean?'

Bill tsk-ed and headed for the spare bedroom.

'Grandad?'

The old man shrugged his bony shoulders, pulling the door shut behind him.

Joe walked, absently, to CJ's study, a sacrosanct space of green leather chairs and matching mahogany desk, book-cases and cabinets, and the cool gadgets he'd loved to play with: his camera-lens mug, vintage-camera pencil sharpener, cinder-block magnets on the message board. He pictured CJ sitting in the squeaky leather chair, sucking on a biro — he often had ink on his tongue — peering over towards the framed wedding photograph that sat between a vase of long-dead daisies and a large bottle of TCP. Joe eyed the square of dust where his PC usually sat. He wondered what the police were really looking for.

He began to leaf through the papers stacked in piles on the desk. Telephone bills, junk mail, old newspapers. The only thing of interest he found was some headed A4 paper for CJ's business in Spain. IFX – Inter Foreign Exchange.

He walked back to his room and opened his MacBook. He typed rapidly: 'IFX Spain', 'IFX CJ Arms', 'CJ Arms finance Spain'. Nothing. There was no digital trail. No electronic footprint. It made no sense.

But a load of stories about the crash came up.

. . . Charles Jesse Arms, known locally as 'CJ', is believed to have lost control of his car while travelling north on Coldwater Road in Derbyshire, in the early hours of 1 January. The 59-year-old's Land Rover crashed through the wall of Slow Mile Bridge into the nearby Jawbone Lake. Mr Arms, from Ravenstor, ran an international finance firm based in southern Spain . . .

. . . Derbyshire police said they had received an anonymous call – from a public phone box in Ravenstor – just before 3 a.m. on New Year's Day . . .

. . . The caller is being sought by officers. Detective Inspector Vincent Slater commented: 'I would urge this individual to come forward. She may know vital details which could assist the ongoing investigation . . .'

. . . Anyone with information should contact Derbyshire police by calling 101, quoting incident number 9 of 1 January . . .

Who was she? he wondered. Maybe she was involved. Maybe she caused the accident. There were multiple sets of weaving vehicle tracks across Slow Mile Bridge, the police said, but probably caused by drunk drivers travelling to and from New Year's Eve parties. Maybe that was it. She'd left CJ to drown because she was drunk or drugged up, or driving without a licence.

Joe walked downstairs to find Eileen watching the TV with the sound muted. An empty wine bottle lay on the floor beside her. She was in her slippers and dressing gown, damp hair swept back from her face.

'Where's Grandad?' he asked.

She sighed, taking her time. 'He's having a lie-down upstairs. He wanted to go home, be on his own, but he didn't want to bump into anyone he knew.'

Joe went into the kitchen. She hadn't touched the sandwich he'd made her earlier. He switched on the kettle and remembered her unwrapping fish and chips to put on plates – a Friday-night thing. She's humming a song, arranging salt and vinegar, ketchup and HP Sauce on the table. CJ insisting on a pickled egg.

She was always in the kitchen when he was growing up, baking, kneading, frying, whisking. She grew her own herbs, and would often ask Joe to go out into the garden to collect a handful of parsley or thyme or mint. They always had guests round for Sunday dinner when CJ was at home.

He went back in, passed her the coffee, and sat in the chair next to her. He eyed the enormous Christmas tree in the corner of the room. It looked like some camp, uninvited guest. He wondered if he should take it down.

She replaced the coffee for her glass of wine. 'I never thought we were going to get rid of that copper this afternoon.' Her voice barely louder than a whisper.

'Grandad said something to me this morning.'

'What about?'

'About Dad.'

Their eyes locked.

'What about him?'

'He said there's no such things as accidents.'

She chewed on her lips. 'And that's meant to be helpful, is it? He's just being his usual annoying self.' She got to her feet.

'We need to talk, Mum.'

She took the pack of Menthols from her dressing-gown pocket, lit a cigarette with the one she was already smoking, then sat back down.

'Why did the police take Dad's computer?'

'You know what they said.'

'Do they think something suspicious has been going on?'

Eileen shrugged. 'You know as much as I do.'

'And you've still no idea where he was on New Year's Eve?'

'CJ just said he was going to the golf club.'

Joe sighed. 'But Slater said they had interviewed all of the staff. No one saw him there that evening.' He paused. 'Do you know something I don't?'

She glanced towards the window. He followed her eyes, expecting to find somebody looking in.

'Was everything OK? Between you two, I mean?'

'Yes. Why?'

'I don't know. It's just some of the questions the police have been asking.'

'Like what?'

'About what was going on inside Dad's head. His state of mind.'

'If you mean was he suicidal, then you don't know your dad.'

'Was he having problems at work?'

'Oh God, I stopped asking about his job years ago. I don't know. Maybe.'

'Why *maybe*?'

'You're joking, aren't you? International finance? It's beyond me, duck. I'm the one who likes to come home and talk about how my day has been. Not CJ. He'd go into a mood for days if something happened at work. I used to try to talk to him about it, but he'd clam up. Talking about it just makes him more stressed.'

'Was he stressed a lot?'

'He just needs peace and quiet. He sits in his study for hours until he sorts things out. I never push him.' She stubbed out the cigarette. 'His comings and goings,' she said, 'they're just part of the rhythm of our life. I don't really know what goes on in Spain.'

CJ's income had leapt over the years. They moved into the 'big house' – a detached, five-bedroom Georgian property, the largest on a well-heeled street, when Joe was just a toddler. The entrance hall with its oak floors, panelled walls and cloak cupboard was almost as big as their former living room, but for Joe the 200-foot-long garden was his favourite place, with its fruit orchard and summer house and stone fire pit. That was before he discovered computers.

Bill's mortgage was paid off. Eileen got a new car every spring and the family always had two weeks abroad every summer, usually somewhere exotic – Mauritius, Thailand, the Caribbean – although often down to Gibraltar. Joe and Eileen never wanted for anything, though CJ was hardly what you would call ostentatious; there was no discrepancy between his income and his lifestyle.

Eileen stared tearily into her glass. 'He wants to retire in a couple of years. He's serious about it. He says he wants to spend more time at home with me. He wants to go on a round-the-world cruise.'

Joe could picture them both on deck, tanned and tipsy, colluding in laughter and private jokes about the other guests.

'He was a right little so-and-so.' She was starting to slur. 'I remember him at school, always getting in trouble.' She liked to reminisce when she was drunk, pausing to remember, trying to end her monologues but never quite making it.

'He left at sixteen, you know?'

'I know, Mum.' He reached over and took her hand and she smiled, squeezing his fingers.

'Just after George died. He disappeared off the radar. Went down to Hastings.'

'Who's George?'

'What?'

'You said George died.'

'George. George Fern.'

Joe didn't recognise the name. 'What happened to him?'

'He was Dad's best friend.' She sniffed. 'They used to go climbing together. He fell from High Tor. His father still lives over in Musdale.'

Did he know this, or had he just forgotten?

'CJ was in Hastings for eight years. I never stopped thinking about him. He came back and we fell in love.'

She let go of Joe's hand and sighed.

'I know a bit about Hastings,' Joe said. 'Dad used to tell me.'

'What about it?'

'The place he ran, the picture house. Empire X. They showed adult films, didn't they?'

A wry smile crept across her face. 'Dirty sod.'

CJ had a passion for film, film noir in particular. Joe remembered countless afternoons watching old films and Super 8s in the darkened living room. Joe loved the soporific sound of the projector, the flicker as the celluloid spooled through the gate, the heat from the machine and the loud, breathy noise it made. Images of the family projected onto the white wall. CJ used to talk about the cinema nostalgically, about how he loved working the projector of an evening. It was the first cinema on the south coast to have stereophonic sound and air conditioning. In its heyday, it had lush balcony seats and enormous black-and-white film posters on the walls. CJ kept some of them. He used to joke with Joe that they sold ice cream during the intermissions.

Joe said, 'But that's about it. Dad never really talked about it much, did he?'

Eileen opened her mouth; he could almost see the unspoken words hovering in her cigarette smoke. She reached for the remote and they both stared at the screen as she flicked through the Sky channels.

'Joe,' she said slowly, 'CJ told me that you're thinking of selling the business.'

'Yeah. Though I'm more than just thinking about it.'

'You don't have to leave though, do you? Go back down to London, I mean.'

'I'll stay as long as you need me, Mum.'

Because I've got nothing to go back to, he wanted to say.

She ran her fingers through her hair. 'Good.'

He jolted himself awake. Eileen was asleep on the couch next to him. Hail glanced heavily off the window – a hollow, percussive sound. The wall clock said it had just gone midnight. He switched off the TV and helped her up the stairs and onto her bed, arms out by her sides. He watched her sleeping for a while, eyes moving rapidly behind the shells of her lids. He wondered what she saw in there.

He scanned the room. He thought it was just untidy, but then he realised CJ's clothes were laid out everywhere. Empty shapes, waiting to be filled.

He pulled the duvet over her, and then picked up a framed photograph from the chest of drawers. The image showed CJ and Eileen sitting around a small wooden table outside a bar somewhere in Thailand. Their second honeymoon, they called it, taken after Joe had left home to go to university.

Eileen's face was a chimera of times past, her lips pulled tight with that brilliantly loud laugh of hers, laughter that always made Joe feel incandescent inside, like his veins ran with lemonade.

CJ was looking at Joe directly in the image.

Find me.

SHE PITS against the cold. Flakes fall like feathers. Behind them, Rabbit's face becomes a blank disc. The forest is a tangle of bark. Chewed by the frost, it resembles concrete. The snow gathers and glitters so hard, so white, it bruises her eyes. I'm dreaming, she tells herself. It's New Year's Eve and I'm running away from the lake. She watches her breath rising. Hears a noise, turns. All she can see is her own set of footprints in the snow, but there is a sound in the sky, like a water pipe stuttering. The flush of adrenalin makes her light headed. She runs faster, stumbling, and though she doesn't look back she knows that he is following her . . .

Rabbit sat up in bed and rubbed her face. She glanced at the empty cot before looking back towards the gap in the curtains, at the patch of sky filled with large pixels, the type of snowflakes that stick to everything. With the snow closing in outside, she felt safe here in her cocoon with Cass.

She was on the late shift. She had to get on with things.

She eyed the black bin bag at the foot of her bed, containing the clothes she was wearing on New Year's Eve – the chequered trapper hat, the green coat with the furry hood, the purple skirt, her favourite Ugg boots and stripy leggings.

She walked over to the window. Fog was sitting in trees, in the outwoods on the brow of the hill that led onto Cuckoostone Moor, so vivid in their whiteness. It was no good hiding. She had to get out.

Blowing into her hands and jigging from side to side, she scraped the ice from her car windscreen. Cass was watching her from the living-room window, a pink figure in the window of the pebble-dashed house.

She drove to the lake, and stood on the shore, hands in her pockets, staring out. The lake's surface held the sky, cloud formations seen through the filigree of bare branches. The gap in the bridge wall and hole in the ice were still visible, the blue-and-white scene-of-crime tape fluttering in the breeze. No police officers to be seen. A sudden break in the clouds, sunlight glittering off the lake's surface.

She heard the snap of a twig, a rustle. She turned and stared into the darkness of the trees, waiting. It was CJ coming back from the dead, dripping wet, covered in weeds. *Why didn't you save me?*

She couldn't stop it. What she had witnessed at the lake that night, it had changed her. Visceral. All-consuming. Anxiety that heightens your senses to a point that's almost painful. She knew that the bad things would find her. She could feel eyes on her at times, eyes she couldn't see. Watching the house. Watching her walk down the street.

How DIFFERENT the world seemed when she stepped onto that factory floor. The morning shift, delirious with boredom and fatigue, looked elated to be liberated from their machines. She spotted Angie, the town gossip, joining the opposite line. They mouthed hello.

How long did it take? Ten, fifteen minutes before she realised it was happening again: moisture under the hard hat, under the stiff collar, a sheen of it across her back, trickling between her breasts and down the insides of her legs into the white rubber boots. The system flowing, ice cream flowing, sweat flowing. The machines without memory, without fear. Machines made elsewhere, their parts assembled in similar factories by similar means and similar people working on a multitude of lines, each with an individual task and skill, swearing under their breaths: just think of the money, nothing but the fucking money. One eye on the line, one eye on the hands of the clock. At times, the second hand appeared to be stuck. 1,440 minutes in a day. 480 wasted here. She tried to quell the panic.

Her arms moved like a dancer's but her mind had left

the building. Mental arithmetic. Rabbit liked to run numbers in her head, breaking her life down into units of time, integers of moments wasted or time well spent. Give her a number, any number, and then another. Ask her to multiply the numbers or divide or subtract and then add another sum on top, and maybe even another. Quick as a flash she could tell you where it was leading. Like she didn't even have to think. As a young girl, her party trick was to ask somebody their age and then tell them how old they were in hours, and then minutes.

She spent on average eight minutes a day brushing her hair, just to get rid of knots, so that she could tie her hair neatly under the factory hairnet. Knots had always been an issue. Some of her earliest memories were of Cass or her mother brushing her hair out after bath time.

Small acts of tenderness. Memories she didn't like to ponder.

Eight minutes multiplied by 365 days multiplied by thirty-two years equalled 93,440 minutes. Plus the forty-eight minutes of leap years. Just over 1,558 hours spent brushing knots from her stupid bloody hair.

In this manner she calculated she had wasted four months driving to the factory (the exact same amount of time, she guessed, she was wishing she were having sex). Eight point six years asleep. Three months singing along to adverts. Sixteen days clutching hot-water bottles and eating chocolate to ease period pains. Almost a full twenty-four hours circling the things in magazines that she'd like to buy when she got a place of her own. Three days painting nails and plucking eyebrows. Two point five days deciding she had nothing to wear and trying to decide which handbag to use. Seven days wondering if she would ever fall in love again. Twelve hours staring into empty cupboards. Six months watching *Coronation Street* and nearly two days having her bits waxed.

It was no good. Today all she could think about was the body in the lake, the figure on the bridge.

Just over a week since she'd seen CJ crash through the bridge wall. Enough to put a distance between then and now, but it wasn't. The events of New Year's Day stalked her like a shadow.

Making the box from the flat-pack cardboard as quickly as possible, a few deft twists of the wrist, arms shuffling, spread fingers pressing the lids onto the charging gush of tubs, she then lifted the tubs into the box, stacking them neatly inside as they got heavier, heavier. Box full, she would push it under the tape machine hoping to God that it didn't stick because before you knew it the ice cream would be all over the floor, they'd have to stop the line, and her line manager would look at her as if she was a worthless piece of shit.

She eyed the clock on the wall, aware of her body moving in some robotic rhythm she'd come to adopt as normal. She cracked down the lids and lifted the tubs while the machines hummed their song, *whirbangbang-whirbangbang, chugplop-chugplop* . . . She closed her eyes as around her the system flowed. Hypnotised by the choral chant of the machines, Rabbit flowed.

'Talking to yourself again? The men in white coats'll be after you.'

It was Frankie.

'All right, knobhead?' Her ice-breath drifted towards him. She was so cold her face was numb.

Francis – though don't ever call him that – wasn't much to look at: perma-scowl, tattoo sleeves, Kappa tracksuit and green stain on his index finger from his faux-gold sovereign ring. When Frankie smiled his snaggle-tooth smile, you saw nothing but brown decay.

They were both council-house kids and in Ravenstor that meant something. Nether Tor – or as the locals called it: Neanderthal – was a seventies sink estate situated on the steep, wooded outskirts of the town, hemmed in by two A-roads, the bleak Cuckoostone Moor, and Musdale, an overgrown valley of ruined watermills, ponds and bleaching vats. Beyond that sat Jawbone Lake.

Frankie worked up on the gantry of the minor ingredients mixer. She often watched him up there, sitting on the thin lozenges of sugar and whey powder, waiting for the bleeps from the computer demanding ingredients for the next mix. He always pre-empted the computer and prepared the bags beforehand. It wasn't diligence; it simply gave him longer to sit on his skinny white arse.

He told Rabbit that most of the time he was careless with the mix, with the percentages of liquid concentrate and the colours and flavours that follow the powders. He told her that sometimes he smoked a joint up there, hiding behind the big cauldron, tapping the ash and flicking the burning roach down into the mixing machine. Most of the operatives didn't eat ice cream any more; they'd seen it scooped off the floor too many times; seen too many fingers going into it and licked clean. They'd done it themselves.

'Shite,' Rabbit said, 'I'm bored out of my skull.'

'I know. Thank fuck it's Friday.'

With a few expert twists of the wrist, she made another box from the flat-pack cardboard. You couldn't stop the flow; the machines wouldn't let you. You could talk as much as you wanted. You could shout and scream and gibber like a fucking idiot just as long as you didn't interrupt the endless gloop. Frankie began constructing a few boxes as they talked, making a tall stack on the table next to her. It would make her life easier for a few minutes.

Break time. Rabbit rubbed her sore neck. A flash of colour in the corner of her vision; she turned – Kate was moving down the line towards her. She worked the twilight cleaning shift, which meant Rabbit only saw her every other week.

Kate smiled; Rabbit blushed.

Frankie shouted down from the gantry, 'Show us your tits, Kate.'

Kate flicked Frankie the V and grabbed a stack of white tubs. She smiled at Rabbit again before disappearing from view.

Occasionally Kate would walk by, squeegee- or bucket-laden, and let her eyes linger on Rabbit. Snagged by the hook of her eyes, Rabbit tried to look away.

After the shift, she waited for Frankie in her car. She revved the engine to create some heat, watching the operatives pulling out of the car park at speed. A Magic Tree hung from the rear-view mirror. The panic was subsiding, but still there – a background pulse that threatened to take over. She wiped the condensation from the windscreen. Frankie walked into the beam of her headlights arm in arm with Kate.

Rabbit glared at Frankie as Kate shuffled onto the back seat.

'What's up with you?' he asked. 'You've got a face like a wet weekend in Wigan.'

When Rabbit didn't respond, he said, 'I told Kate she'd be all right for a lift. Don't mind, do you? She lives up on the tops. The posh end.'

Rabbit was happy saying nothing as she drove, but Frankie kept asking stupid questions. He made one ugly cupid.

'So what you doing Saturday, Kate?'

'Nothing planned. Why?'

'Do you fancy a few at the Crow? Should be a laugh.'

Kate leaned between the front seats. 'What do you say, Rabbit? Sounds great.'

Rabbit could smell the chewing gum on Kate's breath. Going out? The pulse quickened. No.

'Aye. Good. Yeah.'

Frankie poked Rabbit in the ribs and laughed. 'The weekend's here. I best skin up.'

Stepping through the front door, hearing the TV blasting from the living room, she realised she'd forgotten to get Cass's supper.

Despite the generation gap, Rabbit and Cass were more like sisters than niece and aunt. Rabbit's mother died when she was ten years old. Cass had raised Rabbit as her own.

Cass's hair, the colour and texture of straw, was swept back from her face with wet-look gel, and her strawberry-and-cream complexion was mottled a deep and frustrated pink. She had orange crumbs around her mouth and Rabbit noticed the empty packets of Monster Munch on the floor.

'Bit later than usual, aren't we?' she said.

'Dropped Frankie and his friend off first.'

Rabbit was suddenly self-conscious. Cass didn't like her smoking weed. Drinking, of course, was different.

Cass gazed at her with a level of scrutiny. 'A girly friend?'

'Someone he's pals with. You eaten?'

'Thought you were getting me a fish supper?'

'I forgot. Sorry. It's been one of those days.'

'Well, you best get your fanny switching in that kitchen.'

Neither of them moved.

'You feeling all right?'

Rabbit shrugged. She unzipped her coat, finger-combed her long blonde hair, and stifled a sigh. She walked up to her bedroom, and over to the window. Snow fell on the estate. There was no sign of life out there apart from the blue and orange LED flicker of a neighbour's Christmas lights, strung in no discernible shape, flashing in no discernible order across the front of their house. They should have taken them down by now.

She waited until she heard Cass go to bed, and then she crept downstairs, got a bottle of wine and headed back up to her room.

The house was painfully quiet. She placed the bottle on the windowsill but didn't open it.

She thought about Jawbone Lake, about her son's ashes. It felt wrong to be remembering him with this secret inside of her. She'd read the papers, she'd heard Angie's gossip. They knew nothing.

Maybe CJ would still be alive if she'd had reception on her phone and made the call sooner. She'd probably made things worse. Cass, the Arms family, the police, the townsfolk

– they would want to know why she'd stayed silent. What was she hiding?

She'd replayed the image of the Land Rover sliding through the ice so many times it felt embossed in her mind. As if she could reach inside her skull and touch it. As if she could run her hand over the memory.

GROGAN DROVE back to Ravenstor, the radio tuned to the local station. Enough time had passed, he decided. He drove to the lake, parked on the brow of the hill, and eyed the scene. The police cordons still stood, but there was nobody around.

He scanned the reflecting plane of the lake. The sky above was thick with snow cloud, the hillsides across the lake dark like humanoid silhouettes, ice the colour of steel.

The water was too cold for decomposition. They would have to wait for the thaw, for CJ to float to the surface.

He hadn't killed him with a bullet, he knew that much. Not at that speed, that range.

With a hooked finger, he lifted the window button on the car door and the glass slid down with a whirring sound. He spat onto the pavement next to him.

Week Two

JOE WOKE to the sound of snow sliding off the roof. When he looked through the curtains, he found a fresh layer had fallen during the night. Dawn had yet to break but he could make out the snow-capped trees at the foot of the garden, blue in the moonlight.

His head ached. He still woke up some mornings with something like a hangover, a moan in his veins, but he hadn't touched a drop for months.

He lay in bed and checked his emails. He was hoping there would be something from his ex-girlfriend, Sarah, but there was nothing. It had been six months since they'd last spoken. She'd always got on with CJ. On his drive north, he'd sent her a short text message, to let her know what had happened, where he was. Tumbleweed.

There were a few emails from friends in London, saying they were sorry to hear the news. One acquaintance, whose father had died a couple of years ago, said he understood what Joe was going through. Joe didn't believe him.

Relatives and family friends had begun to come to the house regularly to offer their platitudes, as if desperate to share the pain. Joe wanted to tell them all to piss off. Grief, the kind of grief that he was experiencing, wasn't an internal thing; it was external. It was an ache in the walls, a vibration in the floor, a dreary tone in the air only he could perceive. Outside the house, grief had no resting place – it was in the shadow of every tree, cloud, lamp post, building, and he felt the shadows accumulating, mingling with his.

He wandered downstairs to find himself alone. Eileen hadn't come home last night. She had been spending more and more time away from the house, often at her friend Janet's place along the street. He took a shower and then shaved his face and head and examined himself in the mirror; he looked older than he remembered. He was starting to get a paunch.

He had been weightlifting since he was young. He started knocking around with an older boy from Nether Tor called Duff when he was thirteen. Eileen got tough on him that summer; she said he spent far too much time at his computer and kicked his arse out of bed every morning and told him to get some fresh air into his lungs. Duff was the hardest kid in school. There was a rusty bench and a set of free weights in his back garden. He got Joe into bodybuilding. It was a weird friendship and didn't last very long, but it changed the way kids treated him. Until then, Joe was just the geeky rich kid. Easy pickings.

His parents reacted to his muscles in different ways. They were pleased he was no longer a weed. 'Filling out', Eileen called it. He'd catch her looking at him and she'd make some comment about him needing new clothes. CJ, on the other hand, was strangely competitive – squeezing his arms, constantly trying to engage him in battles of strength.

He pulled the ladder down from the attic and climbed up into the dank, chilly space. A cobweb brushed against his head as he stepped across the beams searching for the light switch. The dim bulb illuminated boxes piled on sheets of plywood beside the chimney breast, some of which contained items from his childhood, which he ignored.

The first box he opened was full of old Christmas decorations; the second, old books; the third, VHS cassettes. Then he found it: a small trunk containing three of CJ's old Super 8 cameras and some dusty film reels. Most had garishly coloured cover designs: 'A Royal Decade 1955–1965'; *Carquake* starring David Carradine; a 'Speedy Gonzales' cartoon he remembered watching as a kid; and *Silver Streak*, featuring Gene Wilder. Among these were four reels in plain brown boxes, films that CJ had made.

He pictured CJ poised behind the camera, directing him and his mum into staged positions, shooting them, framing them. Holding the camera like a delicate bird in his hands, a bird no one else could touch.

But CJ must have shot hundreds of these short films over the years. Joe searched for more of the plain boxes, and then the projector, but all he could find was a long thin box containing a projection screen: *Da-Lite. Perfection in Projection since 1909*. Beside it, old film posters in cardboard tubes.

He searched his parents' bedroom, the garage, and then the summer house at the back of the garden where they often stored things. But even if he had found the projector, he wasn't that comfortable using it. Loading it was such a faff, and if you did it incorrectly, the heat of the projection lamp would melt the celluloid.

He found a company online that transferred Super 8 onto DVD using something called the Telecine process. He pressed the number and spoke to a very earnest man about the film cartridges. The man reassured Joe that they wouldn't be damaged or lost and that he would have the DVDs back to him in the next few days. Just before he hung up, Joe ordered a Super 8 film cartridge for himself.

Rabbit and Cass were back in the swing of things. Something seemed to have given between the two women, a slackening of tension, of ill feeling.

'Look at that face,' Cass said, 'long as my arm. You'd think you never got fed.'

'I'm proper chomping.'

'It wouldn't kill you to make something for yourself once in a while.' Cass smiled at her. 'I'm off down town to pick up a few pieces.'

'There's some money on the table for you.'

'Cheers. It'll pay for the wine you pinched.'

'I never even opened it. It's still in my room.'

'Maybe you could put a few posters up this afternoon,' Cass said. 'If you're not too busy, that is?' She winked. 'That bloody cat's got to be out there somewhere.'

Rabbit nodded.

Cass stared, chewing the side of her mouth.

Rabbit asked, 'What now?'

Cass jerked her chin, her eyes on Rabbit's breasts. 'They still hurting?'

Rabbit nodded. 'Be careful out there, the streets are icy. You'll break your neck.'

Cass smiled, walked out. The front door slammed. Rabbit switched the central heating on. She walked back upstairs. While running a bubble bath, she undressed and stared at her body in the bathroom mirror.

It had been seventeen weeks since he'd died and yet her nipples were still dark and engorged, and stretch marks slithered across her stomach. It felt like some joke, the way that he was gone from the world and yet there she was, left with the physical reminders of his arrival.

Midday, she got in the car. The speed with which she drove along the Brian Clough Way dizzied her eyes. She was glad to be out of the valley. Usually, it was a refuge; oftentimes, it felt like a cage.

She dumped the black bin liner in a charity-shop bin, and walked into a hairdresser's. The stylist tousled her hair. 'What'll it be, duck?'

'Don't care,' she said. 'Just need a change. Something completely different.'

The stylist frowned, humming in his throat.

Rabbit said, 'Chop the lot off.'

'Seriously?'

'Yeah. And change the colour.'

'Lighter or darker?' he asked.

'Darker,' she said. 'Black as hell.'

Frankie laughed when he saw her. 'Jesus wept,' he said. 'Did you get into a fight with a lawnmower?'

'If I want your opinion, I'll ask for it.'

'I'm joking,' he said. 'You look fit as fuck. It really suits you.'

'Where's Kate?'

Frankie let his gaze linger on her a while, smiling slowly. 'You should try to make it less obvious,' he said.

'Fuck off,' she said. 'Want another?'

She headed to the bar and ordered a large G&T for herself and snakebite for Frankie. That's when she saw Kate coming through the front door, removing her bobble hat and scarf. They waved to each other, beaming.

'Wow. You look *amazing*,' Kate said. 'It really suits you. I've wanted to cut mine off for ages but I don't have the face for it.'

'You *so* do.'

'Nah. You look hot. Seriously. It looks so much better darker. Makes you look younger. You remind me of someone . . . shit, who is it?'

Kate removed her coat. Rabbit realised she hadn't really seen her body before; it was usually hidden beneath a factory PVC waterproof yellow rain suit, or the joggers and hoody she invariably wore to work. 'Skinny arse and big tits' was how Frankie described her. She had large green eyes that bled into you, and a full-lipped mouth that made you think about one thing.

Kate peered down at herself. 'What?'

'Nowt. Sorry. What's your poison?'

Three hours later, Kate was staring at her.

Rabbit scanned the bar. She had no idea where Frankie was. Probably in the beer garden.

'I'm a bit twatted, to be honest,' Rabbit said. 'I shouldn't have had that spliff. He always makes them too strong.'

Kate leaned across the table, her eyes shiny with drink. She took Rabbit's hand in hers and rubbed her fingers. Rabbit set her teeth with pleasure.

'Should we get a cab?' Kate asked.

Kate's house was all chintz, doilies and froufrou adornments, a clash of colours and oversized furniture. It looked like a nursing home.

'Why you whispering?' Kate asked.

'Your mum or sister might hear.'

'That old bat's deaf. And my sister's not here. She's in respite.'

'Nice house,' Rabbit said.

Kate raised her eyebrows. 'We moved in at the end of last year. We had this big place in the hills above Bakewell, but after the divorce went through, Mum said she wanted somewhere smaller. Not totally out in the sticks.'

That would explain Kate's slightly clipped tones, Rabbit thought. She spoke like a rich girl, everything tinged with irony. She even laughed like a rich girl, deep and self-assured.

'What's funny?' Rabbit asked.

'Our house was called Janeil Manor. My mum's Janet, my dad's Neil. Tack-o-rama, or what?'

'How old's your mum?'

Kate laughed. 'The decor? I know.'

They fell silent. Rabbit glanced towards the large bay window. They were just down the street from the Arms house. Outside the glass, snowflakes appeared suspended in the air, not falling or drifting, just hanging there, crystallised. She rubbed her eyes and felt Kate shuffle nearer.

'Frankie told me about your son,' Kate said wistfully. 'I'm really sorry.'

'Frankie can be a gobshite.'

'Sorry. He loves you, you know.'

'Yeah, I know. We've been best mates a long time.'

'No, I mean *love* love.'

'Don't talk daft.'

Rabbit's heart was pounding. She felt exhausted.

Kate asked, 'So how come you don't like being called Rebecca?'

'I couldn't pronounce my name properly at primary school. It stuck. I was a bit spasticated.'

'Um, I'd rather you didn't use that word.'

'What?'

'Hannah, my sister. She has Down's. I thought I told you?'

'Sorry.' Rabbit peered around the room awkwardly. 'We're a right pair, aren't we?' she said. 'How many times do you think we'll apologise tonight?'

'Sorry,' Kate said, and they both laughed.

She pulled something from her pocket. 'So, Frankie gave me a bit of weed . . .'

Rabbit couldn't think of anything worse, but followed Kate out into the conservatory.

Kate's what's it called, below her nose. The dip. Cupid's bow. Making her lips even more defined. Her skin was so fine, near translucent, like it had never seen the sun. And the freckles across the top of her nose appeared to change in number. Her nose was small, thin, straight, her chin angular. Features straying from plainness in all the best possible ways. A girl with no piercings, no tattoos. She was wholesome but in a way that was a little sad.

Kate asked, 'What are you staring at?'

'Don't know, the label's dropped off.'

The potential of the moment. Were these the right words? These ordinary words? Would she resist, Rabbit thought, if I just leaned forward and kissed her? I really want to be in love. Have a summer romance. Lying in the fields, swallows and swifts darting in the blue sky above. Would she allow it to happen? Am I misreading everything?

'I like the Crow,' Kate said suddenly. 'A bit grotty, but it's all right.'

'It's a dump. But the karaoke night's all right.'

Her mind jumped back to New Year's Eve. Frankie singing. The walk to the lake. Stop.

'What's your karaoke song?' Kate asked.

Rabbit smiled. 'Umm, I don't know. "Sweet Caroline".'

'I thought it'd be "Rabbit" by Chas and Dave.'

'Very funny. What's yours?'

'"Don't Go Breaking My Heart",' Kate said, as if it were an order. 'It means "empty orchestra", you know.'

'Eh?'

'Karaoke in Japanese. We should go sometime.'

'All right.' Rabbit's mind went blank for a moment. 'So how come you only work the twilight shift?'

'Because I'm studying,' Kate said. 'I'm off back to uni in September.'

'To do what?'

'Speech therapy.'

Rabbit laughed.

'What? I'm serious.'

'Really?'

'Why do you find that so hard to believe?'

Of course she was going to university. Beautiful, intelligent, what could she possibly find in this valley to satisfy her?

'My first degree was in English literature,' Kate said. 'Did I tell you that? A complete waste of time. I ended up working in telesales in Manchester until the place went under. I've always wanted to do something worthwhile.'

'I'm a bit jealous, to be honest. I'd love to go to uni.'

'Did you never consider it?'

'I left school at sixteen. Started work.'

'At the factory?'

'God, no. I've only been there for the past three years. I worked at a primary school for a while. Teaching assistant. Then I had a few part-time jobs, bar work, waitressing, being a table monkey. Then Frankie told me about the factory. Ice cream it was.'

'But Frankie said you're amazing at maths. You could study that. Become a teacher.'

Rabbit shrugged.

'Me,' Kate said, 'I'm not very good at algebra, I can't work out y.'

Rabbit groaned. 'I'm scared of debt, I guess.'

Kate looked up, her eyes sharp. 'Eileen Arms was round here the other night. She's mates with my mum. Her husband was the guy who drove into Jawbone, you know?'

Rabbit nodded, staring down at her hands.

Kate said, 'There's something not right about the whole thing.'

'What do you mean?'

'Him just disappearing. No body and that. I know his son, Joe. Well, I've met him a couple of times. Real hottie. Eileen and my mum are good friends.'

'I thought you said you'd only moved here recently?'

'Dad used to play golf with Mr Arms. CJ. He was a nice guy. A dude.'

Act normal, Rabbit told herself.

Kate reached over and took the spliff from Rabbit's fingers.

'Finish it,' Rabbit said.

'Winona Ryder.'

'Winona Ryder what?'

'Your new hairdo, that's who you remind me of, Winona Ryder in that film, the one in the psychiatric unit.'

As Kate talked, Rabbit tried to concentrate. Her head swam. The pulse quickened. 'Where's the toilet?'

'There's one next to the kitchen.'

Rabbit went into the living room, grabbed her coat, and left.

The air outside was bitterly cold. The roadside slush had been frozen into muddy heaps. She headed across the fields, paths worn through the snow by old women using it as a short cut to the Bingo. Suddenly a group of figures appeared on the hillside, staring down. She jumped with fright, but then laughed; snowmen dressed in scarves and hats.

'Silly cow.'

A barn owl began testing the air in some far-off wood. She stared across the whitewashed fells where she could see the solitary light of a farmhouse, and beyond the fells there hung a silver moon against a backdrop of starlight – that scarred and luminous witness.

'Star light, star bright, first star I see tonight, I wish I may, I wish I might, have the wish I wish tonight . . .'

She squeezed her eyes shut, but all she saw was the image of the frozen lake in her mind, ghosted over with snow. The deathly stillness.

She slid her hands under her armpits to keep warm, and stood there for a long time, shivering, blinking at the moon.

When Rabbit walked into the dark living room, Cass switched on the lamp and Rabbit gasped, 'Jesus.'

Rabbit had fallen over in the dark – her clothes were soaked, and covered in mud. She saw Cass staring. 'Don't start,' she said, her cheeks pinked with cold.

'Good job you're not at work tomorrow.'

'Change the fucking record.'

Cass held something in the air. It was a piece of blue paper. Rabbit recognised it instantly, dashed over and snatched it from her.

'You nosy old *cow*.'

'Sit down.'

'That's my business. Raking through my shit. Is there nowt fucking private?'

'Sit. Down.'

Rabbit sat at the far end of the settee.

Cass said, 'Your knee's bleeding.'

Rabbit stared at the birth certificate for a minute, and then her eyes met Cass's in struggle. 'It's none of your business, Cass.'

'Who was it cared for him while you swanned off back to work, eh? Me. I think I have a right to know. I loved him as much as you did, you know.'

Rabbit set her jaw.

Cass asked, 'Why is there no name under "Father"? Immaculate conception, was it? You the Virgin bloody Mary now?'

'Because he's got fuck all to do with it, that's why.'

'I think he's got *everything* to do with it.'

'I don't know.'

'Know what?'

'Could've been one of three blokes, maybe more. You satisfied?'

'You expect me to believe that?'

'You're the one always accusing me of being the town bike. Rabbit by name, rabbit by nature.'

'Who are they then? Give me the names of all your bloody fancy men and I'll find out myself. I take it he knows he died?'

Rabbit laughed bitterly.

'You're just doing this to punish me, aren't you? But I don't know what I've done wrong.'

Rabbit's face tightened.

Cass held out her hands, palms up. 'Just tell us, duck. I won't judge. Just say his name. It won't go any further. I just want to know. Just say it, please.'

Rabbit huffed and scanned the room.

Cass said, 'I know the registrar, you know.'

'So you think I'd tell the registrar who the father was, and not you?'

'Look, I just don't understand.'

'He's gone.'

'Gone where?'

'He's just gone. All right? Gone.'

Rabbit walked out of the room.

The house was dark, the central heating had just gone off, and it was starting to get cold. Rabbit stared at the empty cot remembering his head moving against her neck, the tiny animal sounds he made. His milky smell, safe, comforting. She closed her eyes and could see him, barely a few minutes old, the black umbilical cord on his distended belly, his puce-coloured, creased face with the down of super-fine hairs, and his perfect little hands with their itsy fingernails.

She knew it wasn't healthy, keeping the cot, but she made Cass promise not to remove it. It had to lose all meaning and become just that: a cot. She wanted the breathing that she heard late at night, his little coughs, to wane, but the act of trying to erase his memory seemed to make his absence more vivid. The cot was always the first thing she looked at in the morning, and the last thing she thought about at night. She couldn't stop looking at it, and kept seeing it in her dreams, dreams that felt like they belonged to another mother. Another life.

Cass knocked quietly on the bedroom door and walked in. Rabbit pulled her legs up to her chest, her face a mess of sorrow.

Cass opened her arms, enveloping Rabbit with warmth. 'Hey now. Shush.'

Rabbit felt her tears wetting Cass's nightgown.

'Hey, what's all this? Shush now.'

They rocked back and forth.

THE BUZZ and bleep of a text woke her. In the milky light filtering through her white curtains, the cot on the opposite side of the room looked blurred, unreal. Propped against her headboard in her fleecy onesie, Rabbit stared.

She picked up her phone. Kate. *Why did you leave last night?*

She thought about CJ Arms. The lake.

She just wanted to stay in bed until summer.

A car started outside. Rabbit's heart jumped. She walked over to the window. The street was empty. It was too much. She had to get out.

Rabbit drove to Jawbone Lake. She felt nervous being there, like it was some kind of dare. She parked in her usual spot on the gravel bank, took the kite from the car boot, trudged along Horseshoe Bay, and peered over at the bridge. Apart from the police tape and the broken wall, it was as if the crash had never happened.

It was windless at the water's edge and yet the tops of the surrounding trees flashed and swayed. Perfect conditions for kite flying.

She recalled the day Frankie gave her the kite, the beam on his face.

'He's a bit young for it, don't you think?'

'I knew you'd say that. Look, I saw it and thought it was pretty, yeah?'

'Yeah. It's gorgeous. I love the tails. The ribbons.'

'Well, I thought that maybe you could put it on the wall, above his cot. He can look at it, the ribbons and that. And when he's old enough, we can fly it together.'

A few days later, they flew the kite at Horseshoe Bay, and Frankie was right; he sat in his buggy, completely transfixed.

Holding it now in her hands, she stood on the lakeshore for a while, just staring out. The lake defined her; it told her who she was. Something about the water helped to contain her, made her feel less alone. But the water had a ditch smell of mud that made her feel dirty. Wintertime, the air here was sweet with the smell of snow and ice, and the astringent tang of pine trees, but now that the ice was breaking up, it just smelled rank.

She preferred it here when the weather was bad. The clement days of summer were worst, with hordes of children out on the water, floating by on tractor inner tubes and rickety rafts. She wondered if any of their parents would stop them coming this summer, scared they'd find the bloated body of CJ Arms.

Silence punctuated by birdsong, a Morse twitter. The occasional echo of voices, ramblers in the woods walking the way-signed pathway on the other side of the lake – ethereal sounds.

She noticed a distant figure standing on the jetty.

She unravelled some of the string. Holding the kite by the crossbar, she flung it up into the air and ran backwards, pulling, pulling, lifting it higher. The edges of the lake reflected her dark figure as she leaned back, standing her ground, the fins and ribbons of the kite colouring the sky above, blood-coloured reflections cast across the lake's surface.

Usually the kite's ghostlike movements set her mind at ease, lifting her thoughts on its invisible currents, dancing the open skies, because this was her meditation, emptying and relocating the shadows of memories, scenes, words, emotions.

Joe stood on the cold, damp jetty, tied to the end of which were a couple of empty rowing boats. The ice had broken around the jetty, and the boats looked so lonely, bobbing and slapping on the choppy, black water. Across the lake, he eyed the crested silhouettes of hills and the flat sweep of shore, and spotted a figure flying a red kite.

He thought about New Year's Day, about the Land Rover crashing into the ice, the ripples ringing the pool of their lives.

He pictured CJ bracing himself for the impact, his hands at ten to two, arms straight and shoulders hunched, face smashing into the airbag as the vehicle began to fill, sink. He imagined the initial roar, waters so cold they erased CJ's thoughts, struggling to release his seat belt, kicking out against the pressure, against the ingress of water, unable to find anchorage, suspended. The weight of the engine tipping the car forward but somehow he managed to gain purchase and escape through a window as the car plummeted.

CJ was floating around down there, through the streets of the submerged village, his jeans snared on a corner of guttering, perhaps, as around him deep-water fish moved through the slow-mo gloom, a layer of fine sediment disturbed by the current, creating a dreamy, sepia effect. A slippery, tea-coloured place trapped in time.

He looked over at the figure flying the kite, watching as it dipped and soared, twisting and dancing in the sky.

She glanced at the surface of the water and thought about the submerged village where her great-grandparents used to live. She imagined the underwater streets of Coldwater village, and saw the open mouth of a fish. Like staring down the barrel of a gun.

'Hello.' A voice came from behind her, startling her.

She turned to find a man standing there, hands in his pockets, watching her. She recognised him immediately. Joe Arms. Her body reacted with a jolt; she smiled at him uncomfortably.

'I didn't mean to scare you,' he said.

She glanced up at the kite, tugged on it a few times, and then turned to face him.

He was bald, handsome, with an open, friendly face.

'Weren't we at the same school?' he asked.

She eyed the lake, shrugged.

'You look familiar,' he said.

'Maybe.'

'What's your name?'

She began edging away, pretending to be fully absorbed

by the kite. What was he doing here? Looking for CJ? She walked for maybe twenty metres, tugging at the strings, before she looked back and saw him walking along the shoreline, away from her. She pulled the kite back down to earth and walked quickly back to the car. She glanced back. Joe was only a dot on the shore now, getting ever smaller. She imagined the not-knowing, the wild thoughts he must be having.

She drove away.

Snow was beginning to fall again when Joe arrived home from the lakeshore. He met DI Slater trudging down the driveway towards him.

'I knocked, but I don't think anyone's home.' He looked at Joe impassively. 'Can we go inside?'

Joe asked him to wait in the living room and headed up the stairs to find CJ's computer on the landing. It must have been returned while he was out.

Eileen was sparked out on her bed, fully dressed. The portable TV was on. The room had been tidied up and the wardrobe doors were opened. CJ's clothes had gone.

'For more ideas on style,' the TV said, 'tune in next week.'

'Mum.'

Her eyelids fluttered and he had a brief vision of her in the future as some sad old widow with only the TV for company, looking forward to an early night, reading a slushy novel by lamplight.

He prodded her shoulder. 'Mum.'

She inhaled through her teeth. Blinked.

'Where have Dad's clothes gone?'

'Barnardo's.' Croaky, sleepy voice.

'You're joking?'

'No, I'm not.'

Joe experienced an urgent burst of heat in his chest.

'Slater's downstairs. He wants to talk.'

She snorted a laugh. 'I know why he's here. He's here
to tell us they're calling off the search. He came round
earlier. They returned CJ's files and stuff.'

'Did they find anything?'

She paused. 'They wanted to ask about the joint bank
account.'

'Why?'

She sat up, palming hair back from her face. 'We opened
it years ago. I'd totally forgotten about it.' She shook her
head. 'I've no idea what's going on any more.'

'What's happened?'

She lowered her voice. 'CJ's been filtering money into it
over the years. Nearly four hundred grand. Yeah, I know.
And the police were round here earlier, asking me about
it. I told them I knew. Nothing suspicious, I said. Four
hundred grand?' She lay back down and covered her face
with her hands. 'We're never going to find him,' she said.

The words cut him. 'Don't think like that, Mum,' he
said. 'He'll turn up.'

He headed downstairs and apologised to DI Slater.

'Is there anything I can do to help?' the policeman asked.

'No. But thanks.'

'And you, how you coping?'

Joe shrugged.

'Well, we've just had some results back from the lab. Are
you sure your mum won't come down?'

Joe shook his head. 'What did they find?'

Slater shifted in his seat. 'There were no mechanical faults with CJ's vehicle, but he had been travelling at considerable speed when he hit the bridge wall. We don't know what or who caused the crash. The dive team completed another search, focusing on the dam wall and filtration system, but didn't find anything.'

Something in Joe capitulated.

'How come I get the feeling you don't think he's down there?' he asked. 'There's no one at the lake any more. It's like you've given up.'

'ANPR cameras picked up your father's vehicle travelling from Sheffield to the Peak District on the evening of the crash. Does your father have any business or friends in Sheffield?'

'Not that I know of. Do you know where he was coming from?'

'They only catalogued his movements for a few miles. He must have used country roads before and after.'

Joe considered the information. 'Are the divers going out again?'

'No. To be honest, dive teams aren't really effective in anything bigger than a tennis court. The lake is a mile long, half a mile wide, and over sixty metres deep in places.'

'So what are you saying?' Joe asked.

'We'll open up what we call a "no body inquest" through the coroner's office.'

'But it's barely been two weeks. You're giving up?'

Slater shook his head. 'There is only so much we can do.'

'And how long will it be before he – you know?'

It wasn't yet possible to pronounce the word *dead*.

'Currently, as the law stands, it's seven years.'

'Seven years? That's ridiculous.'

'The coroner may, and I stress *may*, issue a death certificate after the inquest, but it might be another three to four months before you actually hear anything.'

Joe stood up. 'Thank you,' he said.

Slater shook Joe's hand and left.

Joe went back up the stairs, but Eileen had gone.

He carried CJ's computer through to the study and placed it on the desk. An envelope was Sellotaped to the top of the PC; inside was a letter from the police saying they had created an additional administrator account, without password protection. He checked to see if the warranty seal had been broken. It had, which meant the police had cloned the hard drive. Joe booted up. A five-year-old Dell running XP, it took forever. Joe sighed, waiting.

First, he checked the recycle bin, which was empty. He then accessed the temporary folders. There had been a lot of files deleted back in October, mostly JPEGS that had disappeared into the ether, leaving only their shadow imprints behind, and there weren't any unencrypted or non-corrupt words residing inside the file either.

Joe right-clicked on the screen, accessed View and Details and then Date Modified. He then enabled the Date Accessed check box, to see which files had been accessed after New Year's Eve. There were a few corrupted Excel files. Within these corrupt files, between the mass of encrypted symbols, there were words such as 'insurance' and 'third party', but nothing that looked important.

He then tried to open documents from CJ's email client. Again — nothing.

He shut the computer down and sat there for a long time, thinking.

He left out of the back door, following the narrow lane that ran between neighbouring properties, overgrown hedges and low-hanging trees. He climbed over the stile into the allotment, snaking his way between plastic water butts and fences made from house doors.

The kettle was still warm to the touch. Bill's signature smell of twine, Brylcreem and must hung in the air of the tumbledown shed. His tools were hanging from the walls, beautiful in their own way, organised by length and function, immaculately cleaned and greased. Stacked in neat piles were more of his hoards: empty jam jars; a bale of glossy catalogues; a stack of paperbacks; copper piping; balled-up socks; an array of plugs; and three cardboard boxes on which Bill had carefully written 'Broken Things'.

Joe stared through the window, watching crows darkening the hoar-frosted trees, the sky the colour and brightness of tin.

Bill had become increasingly aloof over the past couple of weeks. They had tried to convince him to stay with them, but he'd insisted on going back home. 'You don't need to worry about me,' he'd said. Keeping his distance.

He eyed Bill's worn armchair. Whenever Joe pictured his grandad, he always saw the old man here, working the allotment wearing his high-waisted trousers and braces, shirtsleeves rolled up as he toiled between rows of runner beans and cabbage before coming back in to rub his stiff fingers over the ticking oil heater.

He stepped out of the shed and checked the sky. Darkness

had almost sealed the day. He rubbed his cold-reddened ears and then wrapped his arms around himself for warmth.

He tried Eileen's and then Bill's mobiles again. No response. He walked back to Bill's place and knocked on the front door but there was no answer. All the lights were off. He checked the Crow – where people openly stared at him – and then some of Bill's old haunts, including the butcher's, where he spent hours gossiping about God knows what, but with no luck.

He trudged through the slushy streets, arriving home to the sound of frantic footsteps echoing down the hall.

Eileen was pacing the kitchen, drunk and livid, speaking in a rush.

'Someone called,' she said, spitting out words. 'She said she was friends with your dad, a friend from Spain. Beatriz. She rang to offer her condolences.'

'Well, that's good, isn't it?'

'What do you think?' she shouted. 'She'd heard the sad news, she said, and wanted to know what was happening with the search.'

'Dad had friends over there, Mum.'

'I know he bloody well did.'

'You've never heard of her before?'

'No. I certainly have not. Have you?'

'No.'

'Why did CJ never mention her?'

Joe didn't have an answer.

'You don't think he was sleeping with her, do you?' Eileen shuddered, dirtied by her words.

'No, Mum. Jesus. You don't think that, do you?'

'I'm such a mug,' she said. 'I should have a handle.'

'Did she leave a contact number?'

'No. I hung up.' Her watery eyes watching him. 'First the money, and now this. Who the hell was I married to?'

'Let's calm down, OK? I'm sure she was just an old friend.' Joe looked at Eileen. 'DI Slater had some new information. He said that CJ was in Sheffield—'

'I heard what Slater said,' she snapped. 'I was sitting on the stairs. And no, I've no idea what he was bloody getting up to in Sheffield. I obviously didn't know that much about him, did I?'

'Mum. He adored you. You were the most important person in his life.'

She eyed him quizzically.

'He really loved you,' Joe added.

'I never got used to him going to Spain,' she said. 'I pretended I did, but there was always this cloud hanging over the house until he was back. I wish I'd said that to him on New Year's Eve. I wish I'd taken him in my arms and kissed him and told him how much I loved him. I wish I'd asked him to stay.' She began to sob, silently.

They were talking about CJ firmly in the past tense now. The accident was beginning to stain their memories, as if CJ's identity was breaking down before their eyes.

'I wake up every morning,' she said, 'and for a second, just a tiny second, I forget he's gone. I wish I could stay in that moment forever.' She glanced towards the Aga. 'You know I was here, in the kitchen, when he came in to say goodbye? He'd just had a shower. I could smell his aftershave. The kitchen was in a state. The radio was on too loud. He seemed eager to leave.

'I can remember the first time he ever kissed me. He

78

was my man. We were so lucky he was part of our lives.' Her chin began to crease. 'What are we meant to do, son? Keep going down to the lake every day looking for him? Wait for the thaw? Hope he . . .'

Joe went over to her and hugged her tight. She was shaking.

'I dreamt about him that night. I dreamt he climbed into bed with me and stroked my back. He knew how much I loved having my back stroked.' A cry broke from her mouth, into his chest. 'It's like I'm having to learn how to breathe again. Breathe alone.'

GROGAN TAILED Joe down to the lakeside. Watched him walk along the shore for a while and then talk to a woman flying a kite. The conversation was short. He appeared to scare her off. She left. Something jolted in his memory.

Grogan slid his car silently from beneath the treeline and followed the Honda Civic back onto the estate. She was young, nervous. He observed her shape, size, gait. Saw her face at an upstairs window seconds after she walked through the front door. Black hair, not blonde.

He sat there for a long time, watching. Put the car into gear.

It was after midnight when he drove back across the moors to the caravan near Dore. He couldn't even get out of the car. He ran through the conversation he'd had last night. Lawrence wanted action, not promises. People knew him by reputation. It was Grogan's fuck-up. No matter how long it took, he had to find her.

He lay awake, waiting for the morning light.

THAT NIGHT, Rabbit lay on her bed thinking about seeing Joe at the lake. She tried running numbers in her head to halt the thoughts, but nothing worked.

She peered over at the photograph on her bedside table, beside the empty wine bottle. It was a picture of her mother when she was seventeen. She had stared at the picture so many times she no longer saw her mother, only her absence. She could barely remember her healthy.

'Joe. He didn't see anything, did he?'

The thoughts in her head kept tumbling. She asked, 'You'd try to tell me, wouldn't you?'

She saw a light come on in the hall, and heard footsteps approaching her door. She didn't care that Cass was outside, probably holding her breath to hear her better. She didn't care that she was talking to herself again.

Cass's footfalls descended the stairs.

'You'd be almost a year old by now. Walking, babbling. Maybe even saying "Mum".'

SIDS, the doctor said. Sudden infant death syndrome. No one used the words 'cot death', though they all knew that's what it was.

Rabbit always made sure he had plenty of tummy time, to help strengthen his back and neck muscles, and ensured he always slept on his back. He was healthy. Happy.

He was four months, two weeks, and one day old when she found him.

3,281 hours.

She remembered the day she found out she was pregnant. Cass screamed blue murder. Don't get tied down. You're barely out of nappies yourself.

Then her thoughts turned to the sound of his cry when he was hungry, so different to his tired-cry or dirty-nappy-cry — that heartbreaking edge of despair. Initially, she'd struggled with it all, but steadily Cass had encouraged her to change and feed him. She remembered cuddling up with him on the sofa, the heat from the gas fire turning his cheeks rosy. How he'd look up at her when he was suckling, wide-eyed, bemused.

She climbed from her bed, opened the bedroom door and shouted down the stairs, 'Cass? Cass!'

Cass appeared at the bottom. 'What's the matter?'

'The cot.'

'The cot what?'

'Help me get rid of it.'

Week Three

SEVEN O'CLOCK in the morning, Joe woke to hear his iPhone trilling on his bedside table. It stopped. He reached over: number withheld. He thought about the Spanish woman, Beatriz, and in the silence, he could hear the blood coursing through his ears.

He got up, dressed, and walked the short distance to Bill's house. He tried the back door, surprised to find it unlocked. He stepped into the kitchen and switched on the light.

'Grandad?'

Just the old-fashioned clock in the hallway tick-tocking away.

He put the kettle on and made a cup of tea. In the living room, piled high with Bill's stacks of papers, he called out again. Silence.

He eyed the stacks. Bill's failure to discard what most people would consider detritus started some years ago, not long after Joe's grandmother died. Magazines. Newspapers. The endless reams of junk mail pushed through his letter box. Bill didn't consider himself to have a problem because he saw everything he collected as being useful, of having personal value; though what that value was he couldn't say. It certainly wasn't what the old-timers in town called *rammel* – rubbish. These enormous bales consumed most of the floor and wall space. Some touched the ceiling. The only room free of clutter was the bathroom for the simple reason he couldn't stand to see any of it get wet.

Joe climbed the stairs, knocked on the bedroom door and pushed it open. Through the corridor of paper, he could see Bill asleep on his side. Joe felt the chill in the room as his grandfather blinked at him.

'Grandad, it's me. I've brought you a cup of tea.'

Bill stirred, pushing himself up with his elbows.

'It's freezing in here, Grandad. Let me close the window, eh?'

'It's you that's nesh, youth, not me. What you want?'

Joe placed the tea on the bedside table. 'I've been meaning to ask you, about what you said.'

Bill leaned over with a grunt and switched on the lamp. 'Park your arse, for Christ's sake.' He took a sip of the tea. Despite the coldness of the room, Bill's pyjama top was unbuttoned and beneath the scribble of white hair, his chest had a sweaty sheen to it. 'I was just dreaming about your grandmother,' he said. 'You interrupted her.' His tone was listless, a pronounced tremor to his lips. 'It were our honeymoon weekend in Blackpool. First evening as man and wife. We went down the pier and sat on a bench together watching the sunset over the Irish Sea.' He winked at Joe and managed a gum-filled smile. 'I can still see that lovely slip of a thing. Such black hair she had then.' He raised a shaking hand to his chin. 'It's cruel, isn't it,' Bill said, 'dreaming about the ones that have passed, as if they were still here? I often expect CJ to come through that front door at any time, kicking the snow off his boots, shouting hello.'

'Grandad,' Joe said firmly, 'when you said to me the other week, that there are no such things as accidents, what did you mean?'

Bill rolled over, turning his back to Joe. 'I shouldn't have said anything,' he muttered. 'Don't worry yourself about it. I only meant I can't . . . I don't want . . .'

'It's what Mum thinks, isn't it?' Joe stared at the back of his grandfather's head. 'That Dad had a stroke or heart attack or something.' When Bill didn't respond, Joe added, 'But she also thinks he was having an affair with some woman in Spain. Beatriz. She phoned the house last night.'

'Andalusia.' Bill enunciated the syllables carefully. *An-da-lu-see-ah.*

Joe waited. Bill's breathing became laboured.

'Let me get back to sleep, youth.' Bill grunted. 'Lock the door behind you, and put the key through the letter box.'

Eileen was sitting in the living room wearing her fluffy yellow slippers and pink dressing gown. She had just opened a bottle of wine. A piece of ash from her cigarette fell onto the carpet.

'Mum,' Joe said, 'let me get you a cup of tea. It's too early for that.'

'Let me be, duck,' she said. 'It's just the one. Don't you worry.' She offered a weak smile.

'There's never going to be a right time to ask this,' Joe said, 'but did Dad leave a will?'

She took a long swig from her glass. 'No. I spoke to his

lawyer last week. She said they'd discussed it a few years ago but nothing had been put to paper. It's going to cause me a whole load of hassle.'

'What do you mean?'

'What do you think I mean? The house, assets, bank accounts . . .'

They eyed each other steadily. She shrugged and then topped up her glass.

'Stop staring at me,' she said. 'There's a parcel on the stairs for you. Came when you were out.'

'Are you OK?'

'No, I'm not OK. Don't ask such stupid bloody questions.'

He kissed her cheek and left her to her Sauvignon Blanc.

Inside the parcel were four DVDs and a Kodak Ektachrome Super 8 film cassette from the Telecine company. A letter explained how disc one had to be edited down to seventeen seconds due to the damage.

He knew Super 8 film ran for three minutes and twenty seconds; that came to just over ten minutes of footage.

He slid disc one into his MacBook. It loaded up immediately. The wind played with Eileen's long blonde hair, the top two buttons of her blouse were unbuttoned and her breastbone glimmered in Kodachrome pinks and blues. She was so pretty. *Go away*, she mouthed, and then said something he couldn't discern. A flicker, and the film ended. Seventeen seconds.

The film must have been shot when they first met, after CJ returned from Hastings. He wondered what the damaged sections would have shown. He watched the film a few more times to work out exactly what she was saying.

Stop pointing that bloody thing at me.

He put in the second disc. A landscape open to the camera. The movie was jerky, tired-looking, the cuts erratic and the exposure looked wrong, but there was a rough, dream-lit grain to the palette. The wind played with the trees along the steep track, leaves glimmering in acid greens and blues.

Something about the shakiness of the film made Joe look closer, slowing the frames down, squinting into the jerk and jostle of the warm, super-saturated colours. They had the look and feel of memory, of dream, and yet an ultra-realness.

He knew the landscape; the 120-metre drop to the River Derwent below, and the three white pods of the alpine chairlift climbing the Heights of Abraham on the opposite side of the valley. High Tor. He glanced through his bedroom window, and there it was, the distant summit sloping down into the far outskirts of town. Why would he film High Tor? He could see it from the study window. Was it just a way to waste a few hours, or hone his skills, or was there something trapped in the celluloid? He remembered what Eileen had said, about George Fern, falling from the tor. Was this some kind of memento mori?

He held the other two DVDs in his hand and stared at them a while, and then put them away in his bedside cupboard.

THE GOLF club, situated high on the moors above Ravenstor, had managed to keep the off-course facilities open all winter, but the place looked deserted. There was no one on the front desk or in the main lounge but music was playing across the bar's speakers. Joe walked over to the large picture windows and stared out across the snowy terrain of the course – the rough, the fairway, it was all just an open white landscape.

A man appeared. 'Jesus,' he said with a thick Welsh brogue. Joe could tell from his face that he knew exactly who he was. 'CJ's lad.'

'Yeah.'

The man shook his head. 'You're his double.'

Joe swept a hand across his bald head. 'Apart from the lack of hair.'

The man laughed.

A brisk shake of hands.

'I'm Dave,' he said. 'The greenkeeper. Sorry I haven't been down to the house yet. How's your mum? Ignore that. Stupid question.'

'Don't worry about it.'

'Can I get you a drink? Tea, coffee, beer . . .'

'I could do with some water, if that's all right?'

Joe followed him over to the bar area and sat on a stool while Dave rummaged in the cooling cabinets. He passed Joe a bottle of mineral water. His hands were shaking.

'Do you want a glass, ice?'

'This is fine,' Joe said. 'My dad was meant to be here on New Year's Eve. But he wasn't. He didn't turn up.'

'I know, son. We've spoken to the police. They've interviewed all the staff.'

'Does anyone have a clue where he was? Any ideas at all?'

Shaking his head, Dave leaned his elbows on the bar. 'No, none of us know. We're all stumped. You're right, though, he did tell us he was coming. We'd ordered in a bottle of Jura for him, especially like. He'd polished off the last one in a couple of nights. He didn't half love that stuff.'

'Did he seem OK to you?'

'What do you mean?'

'Well, he spent a lot of time here. When he got back from Spain, just before Christmas, did he seem himself?'

'Your dad was a real character. The heart and soul. Everyone loved him. Always cracking jokes he was, laughing and flirting with the . . . Sorry.'

'So he was his usual self?'

'Very much so.'

'Did he ever mention Sheffield to you? Or ever bring anyone here from Sheffield, any friends?'

'He always came on his own, Joe. He knew everyone, see. Part of the furniture.'

'Was there anyone in particular he was close to? Anyone who I should talk to.'

'No one who can tell you more than I can. I'm sorry, Joe.'

Joe walked back to his car. It was almost dusk. He sat there for a while, staring through his windscreen at the white-washed landscape, imagining CJ here, happy, living his life. He wished he'd accepted CJ's invites to the clubhouse, instead of mocking them.

What was CJ doing? Where was he going to, or coming from? Why had he lied?

His iPhone rang. It was his lettings agent in London.

'Good news,' she said. 'The credit check came back clean. We just have to complete the safety certificates,' she said, 'and get the inventory clerk in, and then we're away. If everything goes to plan, they could be in by the middle of next week . . .'

He'd contacted the agent at the beginning of December. They'd discussed the type of tenant he wanted – professional; no pets; no young children – and within forty-eight hours, a couple had put in an offer.

It was nice to talk to someone who didn't know what had happened, to be spoken to in that brusque, London manner, verging on rude. Joe thanked her and said goodbye.

He cast his mind back to how his life had been last year. He had become The Man Who Stared Out of Windows, a bored, thirty-five-year-old software designer, watching doughy-faced office workers making their way between the tall buildings outside, envisaging what their lives were like, wondering if theirs could possibly be as thankless as his.

He would wait until noon before taking the whiskey from his drawer, waiting for lightning to strike. His travails in life sorted by that first shot of the day. Things had to change.

He opened the window a little and listened to the warbles, whistles and chatter of starlings roosting for the night in a nearby wood.

Andalusia. Sheffield.

That evening, he watched the remaining two DVDs.

Pixels arranged themselves into patterns on the screen, a montage of tiled mosaics, glazed overlays of geometric forms, grids of horizontal and vertical lines, and dizzying circles. The cuts between scenes were jumpy, erratic. Arabs sitting around a table playing cards. Narrow, chaotic streets. It was the Middle East or North Africa. Men wearing woollen capes with Ku Klux Klan-style pointy hats. A woman staring directly into the camera through the slit in her veil. A group of kittens eating severed fish heads at the veiled woman's feet. A pause, then shots of arched doorways and chandeliers and tapestries on the walls, brass lamps and waiters wearing military-style white jackets and red fezzes. A hotel. It must have been on his parents' trip to Morocco many years back. A palm-fringed plaza. A beach, the sand full of fag ends and broken bottles. A lone, sick-looking camel. Musicians playing on a dais in the corner of the restaurant. As if CJ had been walking around the city all day shooting chance scenes. Joe wondered if a younger, tanned version of Eileen would appear at some point.

Then the colour and light of the film changed dramatically, and the focus was a yacht moored out at sea, not too far from land, and it was either sunrise or sunset because the sky was ablaze, clouds glowing orange and pink, the water pastel blue, dappled with the reflections of the burning sky. The nudge and tip of the yacht. Joe imagined the sound of the water slapping against the hull. The film ended.

He slid the fourth and final disc into his MacBook.

The opening scene made the breath catch in his throat. It was Joe on a swing, aged four or five, waving at the camera. He had red shorts and a yellow T-shirt on that he was sure he could remember. A sudden jump to a scene on a beach somewhere and Eileen was chasing Joe along the shoreline into the edge of the waves. It was sunny and she was wearing a short skirt and black floppy bonnet and large sunglasses. CJ standing over Joe with the camera, filming him making a sandcastle. Then Joe and Eileen are walking at the water's edge, hand in hand, sunlight reflecting off the water. Another pause. A scene of Joe in the living room opening his presents on Christmas Day. He was wearing a Superman outfit and was running around the room with one arm stretched in front of him, red cape flapping.

He could just picture CJ in his dressing gown, hair on end, leaning over a tripod, struggling with the Super 8 and cursing loudly, Joe giggling and Eileen telling them both off.

He heard Eileen calling his name from downstairs. She was waiting for him in the kitchen, pacing.

'Where the hell have you been?'

'Here.'

'I'm worried about Bill,' she said. 'Have you not heard from him?'

He shook his head.

'Me neither. He's not answering his phone and he's not at home. I rang all of his usual haunts, checked the allotment. No one's seen hide nor hair of him. I must have been to his house ten times.'

Joe thought back. 'I last saw him a couple of days ago.'

'At home?'

'Yes. It was early. He kicked me out.'

'Did he say owt?'

'No.'

'Did he seem OK? Was he in a weird mood?'

'No more than usual.'

'He's not been himself recently. He's backing away from us. And it's not like him to just disappear like this. I think he's gone AWOL,' she said. 'As if we haven't got enough on our plates. I'm really worried about him. Maybe I should call the police. Maybe DI Slater could help.'

'Don't,' Joe said. 'I think I know where he'll be.'

Driving to the foot of Stark Tor, with the wind lashing the car and high forest all around, black firs bending like twigs, he replayed the scenes from the Super 8 film in his mind. He parked up and pulled on his woollen hat, flicked on the torch and walked stooped following the circle of light. Bill could freeze to death out here. He came to the waterfall and then the little wooden bridge that led over to the foot of the fells. He could barely keep his eyes open. He gritted his teeth, trudging up towards Stark Tor. Above the wail of the wind, he heard a pair of wagtails call to one another with identical chissicks; the church bell tolling the late hour in the valley below.

Once he reached Stark Tor, he cut across the field, snow knee-deep in places, towards the pine wood known locally as Needle Trees, until he came to the ruins of the old cottage, four sagging right angles of mossy, tumbling stone, circled with footprints in the snow. Place of barefoot summers and pallet beds, the deep woods where Joe's great-grandfather, a woodsman, raised his family.

CJ had taken Joe up to the cottage before, telling him the story of their family. Backwoods people and sawyers. CJ said that Bill visited the cottage a lot, as if he was trying to find something in the ruins. 'Losing his marbles,' he'd joked.

Remnants of curtains hung at the windows where some of the panes were still intact, the floorboards warped and loose, nails rusted through. Joe tried to bring the place back to life, to fill it with colour in his mind. On the floor, in front of the fire, he pictured a sheepskin rug. A lamp beside the old pallet bed. A candlewick bedspread. His great-grandmother standing at the kitchen sink, feet filthy on the earth floor, washing pots and clothes with water she'd carried in buckets from a stream, hung from an old-fashioned yoke across her shoulders. Then all he could sense was the close stench of loam, roots, and the musky trace of Bill in the air.

The fire was smouldering. Joe rubbed his hands over it.

'Grandad?'

Silence.

He walked back over to the threshold and stared out into the shadows where a tree creaked in the wind, and there was Bill bathed in moonlight, head hanging low, axe in hand.

'I thought he'd be here,' Bill said, a drip of snot hanging from his nose.

Joe removed his coat and hung it around Bill's shoulders. 'You'll catch your death out here, mate.'

'CJ. I thought he'd be here. Waiting.'

Joe held Bill's gaze. 'I know, Grandad. I know.'

He took the axe and bundled Bill back down the path. He was frozen solid, shivering uncontrollably. Back in the car, Bill began to cough – thick, hacking barks.

Between coughs, Bill said, 'Something happened to CJ.'

'Like what?'

'Past few years – there's been this – this side to him.' Bill swallowed drily. 'It's hard for me to say this, Joe – I think something was – was going on down in Spain . . .'

His sentence petered out. Joe asked him to explain, but he'd exhausted himself coughing and fallen asleep.

Joe sped down the road. A set of headlights suddenly appeared in his rear-view mirror – sticking close for safety, until he got back into Ravenstor. Then the car disappeared from view.

EILEEN TOOK Bill straight to the hospital when they got to the house. He was too weak to put up much resistance.

A nasty bout of bacterial pneumonia, the doctors said. He was a terrible patient, bolshie and argumentative. He kept saying he was fine, but you could hear his chest rattling down the hospital corridor. His lungs looked like storm clouds in the X-rays.

Joe and Eileen were outside Bill's room, talking quietly after a meeting with the hospital psychiatrist. As soon as the doctors found out about Bill going AWOL, about CJ's disappearance and Bill's recent hoarding, they thought it best to assess his mental health.

'But what the hell does it all mean?' Eileen asked. 'They're not going to section him, are they? Once he's fit?'

'No. They're just concerned he's a risk to himself, that's all.'

'Rubbish. His son is missing. The apple of his eye. Course he's acting strangely.'

'You know there's more to it than that.'

She blew air through her cheeks, pushing hair back from her face.

'As soon as he's settled at ours,' Joe said, 'the duty team want to do another assessment. It's for his own good.'

'Look, if he wants to hoard at mine then he's more than welcome. He can fill the house with all the paper he wants to. It doesn't mean he's mad.'

'Keep your voice down.'

'I can't have him going into one of those places. CJ would never forgive me. If they want to assess him, then sure, they can do it at ours. But we're going to look after him, not the state.'

'Look,' Joe said. 'Everything's going to be fine. Grandad's a tough nut. He knows what's going on.'

She tsk-ed. 'I need a fag.'

He wasn't sure which Bill he was going to get, Truculent Bill or Pleasant Bill.

'Does tha come from Openwoodgate? Shut the door, for fuck's sake.'

Truculent Bill.

The room was unbearably hot and smelled of tea, digestive biscuits and disinfectant. The overhead strip light was so bright it made Joe's eyes sting.

The old man looked beaten. 'Couldn't they find me another room?'

'Why? This one looks OK.'

Bill jabbed a finger towards the door and Joe noticed the dirt from the allotment, permanently ingrained under his fingernails. 'I'm right next to the nurses' station. If they're not in and out all day then they leave the sodding door open and I have to listen to them blathering on. I'm taitered with it all.'

'They're only doing their job, Grandad. It's not a hotel.'
Bill pointed up towards the ceiling. 'There's this blue
light up there. It's on all night. I've been a taxpayer all my
life, duck. Is a decent kip too much to ask?' He extended
his arms for Joe to see. 'Look at the state. Where did they
learn to insert a drip, eh? Fucking blind school? And there's
no TV in here. What am I meant to do, stare at the frigging
walls all day? I'm going nuts. And I'm proper clammed.
I've had no snap all afternoon. Ee, youth. I don't know.'
Bill sighed, a noisy rattle. 'What are we going to do, eh?'
He gazed wearily at Joe. 'And what's up with you? Is there
something you're not telling me?'

'Like what?'

'London? You've not been right for some time.'

Joe felt see-through.

'I mean, you're not happy?'

'No,' Joe said. 'Not really.'

'CJ said as much. Why the hell are you selling your
business? You should have a wife and kids at your age.'

'I'm only thirty-five.'

'And you still don't know your arse from your elbow.
You think that city is the centre of the universe. That money
makes the world go round.'

Joe went to the window and peered out at the mizzling
rain. 'It's a bit more complicated than that, Grandad.'

'No it's not. You've all that money,' Bill said, 'and for
what? You've been single for how long now – a year, two?'

Joe nodded. 'Something like that.'

'You're not gay, are you?'

Joe sighed. 'No.'

Bill was struggling to breathe.

'Do you want me to call the nurse?'

Bill shook his head. 'Just park your arse.'

Joe sat down, waiting for Bill to collect himself.

'You said something to me the other day,' Joe said.

'What?'

'You said you thought something had happened to Dad in Spain. What did you mean?'

Bill eyed him steadily. 'I mean when he got back in December. I hardly recognised him.'

'Why didn't you say something sooner?'

Bill tutted. 'Hear me out. You know the weekend he came to stay with you, just before Christmas?'

'Yeah.'

'Did you not notice anything? Some change in him?'

'No.'

Joe had been over that evening in his mind many times, wondering if CJ had given anything away, anything at all. Sitting on the sofa, blowing smoke rings. There, but not really there.

'It happened to me before,' Bill said. 'When I was twelve.'

'What did?'

'Father left home one day. Left me and Mother and my two sisters. He left one Saturday morning and never came back.'

'I never knew that,' Joe said.

Bill placed a fist on his stomach. 'I still miss him.' He sighed with a rattle and then coughed into his fist. 'Too wrapped up in yourself, that's your problem. CJ looked terrified over Christmas. It was like he'd seen a ghost.' Bill gave Joe a look that he was obviously willing him to interpret. 'If I were younger I'd go down there myself.'

The sentence jangled in the space between them.

'I'd go there,' Bill said, 'and I'd get to the bottom of it. I'd go to Andalusia and find this Beatriz he was palling around with. The one that phoned the house.'

'Dad mentioned her?'

'He was showing me some book or other. Her photo fell out. He told me to hang on to it. He was scared Eileen would find it. Jump to the wrong conclusions, you know. This Beatriz will know something, I'm sure of it.'

'But come on, Grandad, these are only hunches. I thought you knew something specific?'

'No, not hunches. CJ told me he was shutting the business. He told me he was selling his casita. A nightmare, he said. A minefield. The Spanish property market.' He sighed again. 'CJ said he wanted to leave Spain for good. He was sick of going once a month. He wanted to spend more time with Eileen, he said.'

'You should have told us this ages ago, Grandad.'

'I've only just remembered.'

'And there's nothing else you can think of?'

'No. Go into my wardrobe at home,' Bill said, 'and look in the tie drawer. You'll find the photo in there. I've collected too much pain over the years. I can't carry any more. Do this for me. Go to Spain and find out what happened to my boy. Find out why CJ is gone.'

Bill's house was cold. Joe closed the door behind him, and made his way forward, through the stacks. He avoided the stairs, turning left into the living room. He picked up a dust-covered photograph from the mantelpiece. Joe at the age of three, Bill is bouncing him on the end of his foot. Joe laughed so hard he peed himself.

And here's Joe at the age of five. Bill is lifting him up out of Jawbone Lake on a summer's day. He wraps a towel around him and hugs him tightly to his hairy, bristly chest, kissing the top of his head. 'My sunshine.'

Another photo showed Bill and Joe building a Lego Spacebase one Christmas. On Boxing Day, the family drove to Skegness − 'Skegvegas', CJ called it − and Bill took a load of sand from the beach, brought it back, and made Joe a sandpit in the garden.

Bill was one of these men who loved rummaging at the tip. He'd constantly bring bits back to the house. Joe used to love playing with the parts of engines and car radios. He remembered spending Saturday mornings tinkering with odds and ends in the garden, and spending the afternoons in the pub playing dominoes with Bill and his mates. He would always be allowed a sip of his bitter.

Other photos, other memories. Joe at fourteen hanging out with Duff and a bunch of kids on Nether Tor estate. It is twilight and some of the kids are smoking, others kicking a football around. Bill appears, catches Joe's eye but walks on without saying hello. Later, he calls at the house. 'I thought I saw a cigarette in your hand,' he says. 'And I felt sad. Cigarettes are nasty, Joe. They killed your grandmother. But it's your choice. If you do smoke, I'm not going to tell your mum or dad, I won't punish you. I just want you to know that I don't want you to.' Joe wasn't smoking that day, and he never did after that.

He didn't know when it was that him and Bill stopped being such good mates.

Joe climbed the stairs, and stared at Bill's empty bed. The silence of the old house was oppressive.

He opened the window and spots of sleet made it through the curtains, making them twitch with Ouija-like movement. A chill grabbed his body and shook it.

He glanced at Bill's bedside table: the blue lamp, the dog-eared Western, the glass for his dentures. He imagined Bill's long fingernails clicking in the dark, lying there finger counting before easing himself into a new day.

He opened the wardrobe and located the tie drawer.

In the photograph, a young woman was lying on the sand, her skin the colour of mahogany, and her purple bikini was shiny, wet-looking, as if she had just walked out of the sea. Her body cast a wide shadow and she was looking directly into the camera but not smiling. Her pose was unnatural, forced. She was trying to be seductive.

So this was her. CJ's other life.

Joe was shocked by her beauty.

THE DOCTOR said that Bill was making good progress and could be discharged within the next week. After their trip to the hospital that morning, Joe sat in the living room talking to his mum.

Eileen smiled. 'You sound just like your dad at times.'

Their eyes locked.

'We'll have to get one of the spare rooms sorted for your grandad,' she added. 'Can you see to it?'

Joe nodded. 'I'll sort it before I leave.'

'Leave?'

'I'm off to Spain. Fly from East Midlands tomorrow. I want to check on the IFX office.'

'Oh.' She blinked rapidly. 'Why?'

'I need to see it for myself. Talk to people who knew him. See if something was going on towards the end of last year.'

Eileen nodded, chewing her lip.

'Did you notice any change in him?' Joe asked.

'No. Not particularly.'

'Grandad seems to think something was wrong.'

'He thinks to tell us this now?'

'If anyone asks, I've gone to sort Dad's casita out. Have you got the spare keys?'

She looked glazed, staring into space.

'Mum?'

'I put them back in his desk drawer.'

'Did you ever go?'

'No. I went to the old flat in Gibraltar a few years ago, but not this new place. Will you speak to this Beatriz woman?'

'If I can find her. I won't be away too long.'

She took a final drag on her cigarette and ditched it in the ashtray.

After he sorted the spare room out for Bill, he opened the window and peered into the dark street outside. He remembered playing as a kid. Blocky-one-two. Hide-and-seek. Kiss, cuddle or torture with the Carvers and Clarkes and Johnsons and Grants. It seemed like such a long time ago now, the summers in the streets, CJ still alive.

He thought about what Bill had said about going to Spain. *Do this for me.*

Something wasn't right.

He headed down into the kitchen and straightened the chairs beneath the table, trying to remember the last meal they ever shared together.

A SUDDEN screech of tyres. A car engine popping, banging. Rabbit sat up. Headlights flickered under the curtains, then darkness. She rushed over to the window. A car was turning off at the end of the road. A shadow behind the wheel. The glow of a cigarette. 'No one,' she said aloud. 'No one.' The clock flashed 5:17. She swallowed the panic, counted the numbers.

Think about something else. Her mind tracked back to Saturday night. It was just the three of them: Rabbit, Frankie and Kate. They decided to brave the Crow's 'Saturday Night Special'; Frankie ordered one fishbowl of cocktails after the other.

Since the night she did a runner from Kate's, it had been obvious something was unfolding between them. They were spending more time together; pillow-texting late at night; catching each other's eyes at work. They had even gone out with Kate's sister, Hannah, for a pizza. They had gone for drives, away from town, driving away from the gossips.

Rabbit had been in that situation before.

Until now, it had just been furtive hand-holding and cuddling, but yesterday morning Rabbit had woken up in Kate's bed, and couldn't stop herself tracing a fingernail down her hip. Kate brushed the covers aside, and knocked her hand away.

'You need to leave.'

Driving away from Kate's house, entranced by the glare of the low January sun on the windscreen, she felt like she'd betrayed herself. Kate was beginning to open up another part of her mind, one reserved for lust and longing. At first Rabbit regarded these feelings stonily, but over the past couple of weeks she'd allowed herself to get carried away. She already knew these feelings were leading her down a blind alley. So what's the point? Starting over with somebody new. Somebody asking those nagging little questions that at best elicit tired sighs. Questions about your past, your history, assembling a faulty picture of you in their heads, and for what? All of that shit.

I should have known she would react that way, Rabbit thought to herself. I should have just left. It should be Kate feeling like crap wondering what she'd done wrong, wanting to talk it over, talk it through.

She texted Frankie. Back to the Crow to do it all over again.

Pushing the buttons of her blouse through their tiny slits – she looked over at her clock again. 5:20. Jesus.

Up before dawn on a Monday morning wasn't her favourite time of the week, and hangovers didn't usually affect her; she was still young enough to be able to brush them off with a strong coffee, returning to the unsympathetic machine of the factory without too much sorrow. But today she felt like hell.

The morning went by in a blur of daydreams. Rabbit felt the fatigue, the weariness, sweat pouring beneath her scratchy white uniform, under her blue hairnet. She imagined the whole place collapsing around her ears in a fantastic firework display. She eyed the engineers pacing the perimeters of the factory floor, searching for loose details, leaky connecting tubes, looking busy. Wishing Frankie would come down and talk to her. Distract her from her thoughts.

Freezing cold to the touch, the gloop-filled plastic tubs came at her in their endless conveyance. The noise was horrific and all that standing and leaning over the belt was doing her back in. She was definitely tougher than she looked. You needed mettle and will to work the line. But here she was a nobody. No longer a grieving mother. No longer falling for a girl who kept blowing hot and cold. No longer the woman carrying a secret around.

At intervals, the line would stop and she could hear snatches of music coming from the radio and everyone would sing along at the top of their voices as if they were drunk at a party. She would watch the operatives while they worked, some just staring blankly ahead while their arms moved, others talking to themselves and having imaginary arguments. Everyone appeared so alone and yet all part of the same horrible machine.

She mouthed a silent message: 'Fuck, I hate this place.'

*

It was unlike Angie to come and sit with Rabbit in the canteen, an echo-filled place of plastic chairs, stained tables and smelly coffee machines. Her presence usually only meant one thing: she wanted to bitch. She earned the moniker because she was always moaning. She was your common or garden self-obsessed neg-head, only happy when she was miserable. But Morbid Angie was full of pleasantries today.

'So, have you not seen owt of your cat yet?' Angie asked. She had rank tea-breath and poorly shaved eyebrows. She looked a mess.

'Nope. Hide nor hair.' Rabbit wondered if Angie had stolen him.

'I've seen your posters up everywhere.'

'Oh yeah.'

'Daz said he might have seen the cat down near Musdale.'

'Daz is a compulsive liar.'

Angie sighed, shaking her head. This was Rabbit's cue to ask, What?

'What?'

'Oh, nothing. Just something I heard.'

Rabbit folded her crisp packet into a triangle, ignoring her.

Angie continued. 'Something about CJ Arms. You know, the man who—'

'I know who he is. What did you hear?'

'That he was having an affair with some woman.'

'Who told you that?'

'Just something I heard.'

'What else did you hear?'

'Nothing really, just that.'

She was fine. Nobody suspected anything.

Rabbit sealed her lunch box, gave Angie a sarcastic smile, and exited the canteen.

After she finished work at 2 p.m., she dropped Frankie off, parked her car at home and then headed into town. She was walking, eyes down, when she heard Kate's sister, Hannah: 'Rabbit. It's Rabbit.'

Rabbit turned and found herself face to face with Kate's mum, Janet, looking at her with bouffanted loathing. She was wearing a trouser suit. She'd returned to the work-place after twenty years of housewifery and she was quick to let you know about it. She had the pinched, sour face of a woman who had never said anything remotely hilarious in her life, and if she wore glasses, she would have peered at Rabbit over them, her expression a visual tut. Fortunately, Rabbit couldn't see anything of Kate in that face.

Hannah barged between them and grabbed Rabbit's arm.

'Hello, Hannah. How was college today?'

'Come along now, I'm sure Rabbit doesn't want us pestering her,' Kate's mum said.

Hannah hugged Rabbit's arm.

Kate's mum dragged Hannah away, leaving Rabbit standing there, feeling lumpen, so white bread.

She picked up a bouquet from the florist's and then headed to the churchyard. She walked the cobbled path, the high perimeter wall standing black and glistening alongside her. Here and there tall poplars appeared above an understorey

111

of rhododendron. Gravestones marched up the steep field, epitaphs flickering before her eyes, rough as rotten teeth. The dark green swirls of a Celtic cross beneath a towering yew tree. A headstone like pages of an open book, one half full, the other blank: a corpse, waiting for company. The sad-faced angels looked down at Rabbit and Rabbit glared back.

She crouched down and ran her fingers over the words carved into stone.

Anna Jane Miller.

The day she was born, the day she died. Today was her deathday.

Rabbit placed the daisies carefully against the headstone. Cass would be along later today; it was something they had to do alone.

She peered over at the church and felt a grasping, something fixed inside of her, like a pair of hands wringing her heart. Remembering the pews of blinking eyes, Cass's damp hand. Poor thing. Ten years old. What an age to lose your mum.

She stood there for a long time, staring at the headstone.

'Bye, Mum. Keep an eye on him.'

In her dreams – or those half-awake, half-asleep moments – she returned to her in a black-and-white fog, a woman always on the edge of the frame. Rabbit shut her eyes to try and see her better. Thinking about the last days she spent with her – at least in the skewed world of memory they felt like days, though they must have been months – all she could remember was her mother's medicine-breath, wild hair, shaking hands and rheumy eyes.

She shivered. A gust of wind, and a sudden movement on her left. She turned to look, but there was nothing there. The gravestones leered back at her. 'Hello?' Her voice sounded thin in the emptiness.

Stupid, she thought. Stop it. But she could sense someone. Watching. She stood up and traced her path back to the car, counting the steps in her head.

Frankie was lying on his bed in his tiny bedroom. Oversized TV hanging from its corner bracket. A torn, stained Union Jack flag hanging from the wall. Above his bed was a mirror, on which he had stuck a Carlsberg label, part peeled off.

'Jesus, it stinks in here,' Rabbit said.

He pulled his baseball cap from over his eyes and smiled a bleary-eyed smile. He held out his fist. She bumped it.

'Sorry,' she said. 'Were you having a siesta?'

'No, it was just a very long blink.'

He sat up and stretched his arms. Rabbit sat on the end of the bed and tickled his feet, making him squirm.

'I think something crawled up your arse and died,' she said. 'Can I open a window?'

'No. It's colder than a witch's tit out there.'

Frankie was a sun worshipper. Lithe, rangy, his face so drawn he often looked aghast, he'd be out in the sun all summer if he could, his skin turning pink through to red but never brown. Every year he'd escape for two weeks on a cheap package deal with the lads from the estate, and every year he'd return burned and blistered.

Last summer, Rabbit was always worrying about the sun, about those mad flies in the field down near Slate Lick.

The summer in the park with Frankie and him, Frankie with his T-shirt on his head like a play-Arab, pulling faces and making him giggle. Frankie was brilliant with him. He doted on him. Not once had he asked who the father was.

'Are you all right?' he asked.

She nodded. 'Yep.'

He lifted a half-smoked spliff from the ashtray, lit it, and passed it to her.

'Look at us,' she said, 'thirty-two and still living at home. It's sad.'

'I know,' he said. 'But I meant it, you know. We should totally get a place together.'

'Jesus, can you imagine it? We'd be stoned twenty-four/seven. We'd get nothing done. The place would be a health hazard.'

She examined his face, noticing the slight bruising around his mouth and the scratches along his neck – marks made by his psycho mother, no doubt. He gave Rabbit a sheepish look.

She touched his arm and whispered, 'I'm sorry, babe.'

He shrugged.

She climbed off the bed and walked over to the window. The estate was a huddle of orange-bricked boxes, some with immaculately kept, gnome-laden little gardens, but still, for most, that air of borderline poverty.

She eyed a car parked along the street. A silver Mercedes. A figure in the front seat.

'Frankie, come here.'

'What?'

'Just come here.'

But as Frankie slowly clambered up, the car drove off.

He stood beside her, a hand on her shoulder. 'What am I meant to be looking at?'

'Nowt. Don't worry. What time is it?'

'Nearly four.'

The panic rising.

'Do you fancy getting out of here?'

'Why?'

'There's something I want to show you.'

He stretched his arms, cricked his neck.

'I'll take you for pizza afterwards,' she added.

'Go on, then.'

Soon the hamlet would come into view through the wind-screen, a brown huddle in the snow-covered valley below. It felt right. It felt OK. They passed some old mill buildings and an opencast quarry. By the time they reached the row of cottages, the sky was evanescing.

She turned off the engine and wound the window down, the air smelling of moor-top wind, the essence of the Peaks. A street light flickered on further down the street.

Tiles missing from the roof. Windows boarded up. Render had fallen from the walls in chunks. The front door had peeled, buckled. A huge crack zigzagged the pointing, making the house list. Small trees grew from the roof and gabling. Nature assimilating her childhood home, her memories. Behind the house, a crag rose to almost a hundred metres, a sheer rock face that had terrified her as a girl. In her memory, the house was always semi-dark, dank and claustrophobic. Above the crag, the dark moors rolled out of sight.

'I've not been back here since.'

'Why?'

She'd wondered that herself. 'Just scared, I guess. The place is so much smaller than I remember. I'm amazed it's still here.'

'Looks like it won't be for much longer.'

Rabbit said, 'They should have torn it down. Looks dangerous.'

'They? Who owns it? You?'

'No idea. Even if I do, what the hell am I meant to do with it? It's basically a house-shaped pile of rubble.'

'We could do it up. Live together.'

This woebegone place, it had grown so powerful in her mind over the years. She remembered thunder and rain pounding the cottage, crying, just so her mum would cuddle her. 'It's only God rolling coal across the sky, silly,' she would say, and they would both lie on the couch together.

She recalled the first few days after her mum died, moving in with Cass and lying in bed at night terrified of the shadows in the room, not fully understanding what being dead meant. Wondering where her mum had gone.

'I remember the wardrobe in my mum's bedroom, a huge wooden thing that used to belong to my nana. I'd climb in and dress up, surrounded by her scent. Mum would always tell me off if she caught me, but she'd smile, as if she wanted to get in too.'

Frankie chuckled. 'What else?'

'I remember the bright blue carpet, the pictures on the chest of drawers and dressing table, even the cracks in the ceiling. When I close my eyes, I can see them. Like looking at a photograph.'

The buckled, torn linoleum in the downstairs bathroom. The smell of chip fat in the kitchen. The manky tea towel over the chicken carcass on the first shelf in the pantry. Random memories, the texture of her childhood.

The sound of sirens echoed from a nearby quarry.

Frankie was quiet.

'It's the anniversary of her death today,' she said. 'Twenty-two years it's been. Feels like yesterday. If I was to write the story of my life, I'm not sure I'd like it very much. I'd think, What a bloody tragic story that was.'

'I'm sorry.'

She turned to him. 'Why?'

'You looked like you'd been crying. I should've asked.'

She took his hand in hers and stared back towards the cottage.

'This might sound silly,' she said, 'but would you like to come fly the kite sometime?'

'I know you've been going there,' he said.

'Where?'

'Jawbone. You've been going down to Jawbone to fly the kite.'

'You been stalking me?'

'No. I was poaching. Ask Daz if you don't believe me.'

'What did you see?'

He shrugged. 'It looked private, whatever it was. I didn't want to disturb you.'

'My family were from there, you know.'

'Where?'

'Coldwater village, beneath the lake.' She threaded her

fingers into his. 'There's something I need to tell someone.'

'About what?'

After a moment's silence, she said, 'Nothing . . . It's nothing.'

Frankie sighed. 'Well, whenever you're ready, I'm all ears.'

BACK AT the caravan, Grogan washed, shaved, changed.

His pocket started to vibrate. He pulled his phone out and stared at the screen. Lawrence.

'I got your message about Joe.'

'Good.'

'But let me guess, you've no idea where he was flying to?'

'No.'

Silence.

'And you've still no idea who the woman is?'

Pause. 'No . . . Not yet.'

'Find her.' Lawrence hung up.

Grogan opened the cupboard. He needed to be prepared. A highly competent sharpshooter, he knew he could get a headshot of up to three hundred metres with his Remington Model 700 bolt-action 7.62. He also took the Seecamp .32 – a 6-shot semi-automatic, perfect for ultra-concealment – and the Glock Model 19, which could be hidden snugly in his belt holster. He placed extra ammo into his bag, including Glaser Safety Slugs for both guns.

He locked the door behind him.

Week Four

THE HEAT hit him as soon as he stepped off the aeroplane; he expected late January to be much cooler than it was. He hailed a taxi and sweated in its faux-leather seats. They left the industrial dead zone of La Linea behind, weaving slowly up into the foothills of Andalusia. After an hour or so, the taxi driver motioned to Joe. 'Jimena de la Frontera.' A cluster of white houses visible in the distance. Sugar cubes dropped in mud.

They climbed the narrow streets of the town, finally parking on a cobbled street. Joe looked up the road to a Moorish castle perched on top of the hill. He could see the valley below him, lush and green. He pulled a handful of damp euros out of his pocket and paid the taxi driver. He stared at the casita, perplexed. No door. The taxi driver chuckled, pointing at a passageway to the left of the house. The street was strangely quiet. Joe smiled, walked down the passageway and climbed the single flight of stairs.

The casita itself was small: no more than an open-plan sleeping and living area, with a tiny galley kitchen and an even smaller shower room. The ceiling, striped with wooden beams, sloped up towards the bedroom area at the rear, where a large mosquito net hung around the bed like something from the *Arabian Nights*. There were two windows at the front of the casita, both with Juliet balconies overlooking the cobbled street outside.

Joe dumped his bag on the floor, and began searching. Aside from the address, Eileen knew nothing else about CJ's Spanish life. No extra keys, no numbers. He checked everywhere; he even took the flamenco paintings from the walls, moved the electrical equipment around, and felt along the tops of the oak beam and inside the wood-burning stove. The place was devoid of all traces of CJ. It didn't look like he intended going back there.

He sat on the edge of the bed and scanned the room, imagining CJ in this small space, his eyes resting on the wooden plaque on the wall that read: *Falsehood often goes further than truth*, and then on the cupboard under the TV. Inside, he found an expensive-looking bottle of Rioja; a tin containing a pungent wad of marijuana, rolling papers and tobacco; and a Spanish phrase book.

Joe stared at the tin. He never suspected CJ of being a secret weed smoker.

IFX was situated on an industrial estate near the railway station. Signs on the fence displayed vicious-looking Alsatians and Rottweilers, but Joe couldn't see any dogs or security cameras anywhere. In fact, the area was deserted. No one would see him scale the fence or hear the smash of a window.

The place was dim, dusty. His footfalls bounced off the brick walls and around the low ceilings. There were piles of aluminium, chromium and brass, bits of old radios and stereos and TVs and empty suitcases. Bits of people's lives, discarded. BMW and Rover and Mercedes-Benz sign plates, tyres and bits of engines and smashed windscreens. It looked like the scene of a motorway pile-up. But there was nothing in there to suggest that this had once been the hub of a successful international currency exchange. In fact, if it had been an office of some kind, it looked like it had been shut for some time. All that remained was a large desk, drawers opened, nothing inside but dead spiders, dust.

He spent the rest of that hot afternoon showing photographs of Beatriz and CJ to the few people he met on the street and in cafes and bars. One or two recognised CJ in the photograph; they smiled when they saw the picture and nodded, speaking in a fast, lilting Spanish, but nothing Joe could understand. No one appeared to speak any English, apart from the postman.

'Sí. He English.'

Joe nodded. 'Did you know him?'

The man frowned and then pointed up the street towards the castle.

'Casa John. Englishman. He live there. You ask. *Adiós*.'

Joe made the ridiculously steep hike up to the castle which left his shirt soaked with sweat. Partway up the mountain, he saw a street cleaner standing with his trolley and broom. The man stopped what he was doing and observed Joe with a vacant look on his face, his lips moving but no sound. He was shirtless, his body dark and greasy, and he had breast buds like a pubescent girl. Joe bid him an uneasy *hola!* and walked on.

At the top of the hill, he stopped to catch his breath, looking down across the terracotta rooftops towards the Rock of Gibraltar and the distant mountains of Morocco. As beautiful as it was, there was something eerie about the place, especially now, during the dead time of the siesta, when the unnatural silence only intensified the feeling that he was being watched.

He located Casa John easily enough, a single-storey building with tiny square windows. Painted a deep blue, the house looked completely incongruous among the white walls of the *pueblo blanco*. He knocked on the wooden door. He was sure he could hear footsteps approach from within, but the door remained closed. He knocked again. Nothing.

That night he showered, had a light supper, and checked his emails. A message from Eileen. 'Call me.'

She picked up on the first ring.

'How's the house?' she asked. 'Has CJ left anything there?'

'No. The place is spotless.'

'The office?'

'Looks like it's been shut for some time.'

She sighed.

'I know,' Joe said.

'And have you found her yet?' She said 'her' with real venom.

'No. But apparently there's an English guy living in the town.'

'He must know CJ.'

'That's what I thought. How's Grandad doing?'

'He's fine, duck. He's sleeping right now. We actually had a nice day today.'

She sounded so much happier than the last time they spoke. Sober, less tense. Maybe having Bill there for a while was a good idea. He tried to imagine the two of them in the house together, Eileen's smoking, compulsive TV-watching and cheesy jokes grating against Bill's OCD, his incomprehensible woes and diabolical farts.

'We had a good long chat,' Eileen said, 'and he's asked me to put his place on the market. He doesn't ever want to go back there.'

'Why?'

A non-verbal shrug down the telephone. 'You all right, Joe? You sound distant.'

'I'm fine. So he's moving in permanently?'

'I guess. Permanently for the time being.'

At 10 a.m. the following day, he hiked up the mountainside to Casa John. He knocked, stepped back and stared at the house. A movement caught his eye – a figure silhouetted in the window. Joe waved, pointed at the door. The figure vanished. Joe knocked again, harder. There was the sound of footsteps. The door opened. The man who stood there was extremely skinny and pale and had a day-old grizzled beard and piercing blue eyes. He looked ill.

'I'm sorry to bother you,' Joe said. 'My father used to live here in town. I'm trying to find anyone that might have known him.'

'Well, I've lived here nearly fifteen years now, so I guess you've come to the right place.'

'Charles Arms?'

The man frowned.

'Everyone called him CJ?'

'Ah.' His smile revealed a row of perfect, Hollywood-white teeth. 'Yes, I know him. I've seen him at the flamenco nights in La Bodeguita. Why did you say you're looking for people who might have known him?'

'He . . . he's gone missing.'

'Oh. I'm so sorry. What happened?'

'There was an accident.'

'Oh.' The man appeared lost in thought. 'I wonder if Dr Stone will know more. I always saw them together. He lives in the villa at the very bottom of the canyon.'

'Dr Stone?'

'The villa just over the bridge, in the canyon bottom. You can't miss it. I'm really sorry I can't be of more help.'

Joe headed back down into town, feeling like his legs were made of rubber. Old women stood on doorsteps, getting in a bit of gossip before retiring to the dark interior of their houses. They all stared at him blankly, not smiling when he bid them *buenos días*.

He phoned Bill's mobile.

'I've been waiting for you to call,' Bill said.

'How you keeping? You feeling any better now?'

'As good as can be expected.'

'Did you ever hear Dad mention a Dr Stone?'

'No. Why?'

'What did Dad say about this Beatriz woman?'

'Nothing, really. But I think he had a soft spot for her.'

'What do you mean "soft spot"?'

'What do you think I mean?'

Silence.

'Mum tells me you're selling your house,' Joe said.

'Correct.'

'Are you OK?'

'No. I want to know what you're fart-arseing about at.'

'Give me a chance. I've met someone who knew Dad, though. He told me he used to hang around with a bloke here. This Dr Stone. I'm going to visit the house later.'

'Text me the address.'

'Why?'

'Just in case. Don't trust anyone. Be careful.'

'Careful?'

'You heard. Phone me as soon as you've got something useful to say.' He hung up.

FLOODLIT, LA Última Parada was stunning: a hacienda-style villa with gardens that ran down into the canyon. From the road, Joe could see the main house, a curved facade fronted with creamy-coloured almond blossom. He pressed the intercom and a CCTV camera swung into place.

The intercom crackled, '*Hola?*'

'*Hola* . . . um, I'm looking for a Dr Stone?'

The metal gates slid sideways with a clanging sound. Joe stepped onto the gravel drive that snaked between lush lawns, and was surprised by a man striding out to meet him. Despite his clean, neat appearance, Joe recognised him immediately: the street cleaner. He gestured for Joe to follow him.

They walked away from the main house, along a well-lit path beneath swaying palm trees towards a low-slung bungalow set back in the grounds. A wooden ramp led up to the lip of the door.

The cleaner ushered him into an entrance hall where the air con was set to an icy blast. Joe rolled his shirtsleeves down, buttoned the cuffs and coughed loudly, the sound echoing off the tiles.

'Come in, come in.'

Joe followed the voice towards an open-plan dining area. Jazz was playing in the background and there was a familiar smell in the air – roast beef and gravy. Two men shuffled around the kitchen area, staff of some kind.

A figure with his back to Joe rose from the table and turned, his hand outstretched.

'Joe, right?'

Joe nodded.

'Dr Stone. Very pleased to meet you.'

Dr Stone was extremely fat, and yet carried himself with elegance. He had moles all over his face and his nose looked like a pitted vegetable. There was a sheen of sweat on his upper lip.

Joe smiled, shook his hand.

'You look just like him. CJ. But I expect you know that.' He grimaced. 'I was really sorry to hear what happened.'

Joe nodded. 'Thank you. How did you find out?'

'I saw it on the Internet.' He let go of Joe's hand. 'If there's anything we can do to help, at all, please let me know.'

He gave Joe a sympathetic smile. Joe got the uncanny feeling that he had been expecting him to drop by.

Joe said, 'Sorry to trouble you like this, it's just that an English guy in the village said you knew my dad.'

'And which local might that be?'

'The man who lives at Casa John, near the castle?'

Dr Stone's nod was minimal. 'As I said, I was sorry to hear the news.' He continued to stare at Joe, as if taking an inventory.

'How did you meet? Were you good friends?'

'I'm not sure. We probably met at the British bar in town. Or the flamenco night. He was a nice man. He visited occasionally.' Dr Stone gestured towards the table. 'We've just about finished eating. Are you hungry?'

Joe shrugged. 'No. I'm fine. Thanks.'

'What about a bit of cake? Some coffee?'

Joe nodded. 'OK. Thanks.'

Dr Stone clapped his hands together and shouted something in Spanish.

A voice came from behind him: 'And who's this?'

Joe turned round to find an attractive, middle-aged woman rolling towards him in a wheelchair.

'My wife, Rosario,' Dr Stone said.

'Rose, please. And you don't need to tell me who this is. I can see.' She beamed at Joe and then frowned. 'Sorry to hear about your father,' she said. She wore a tight vest top that showed off large breasts and muscular arms. Her handshake was impressive.

Dr Stone ushered them towards the table, 'Sit down, sit down,' positioning himself at the head while Rose and Joe sat opposite each other.

One of the staff served Joe a very large piece of chocolate cake and poured a cup of coffee. There was a protracted silence. Joe nudged the cake with his fork. Dr Stone looked at him and Rose in turn.

'So how are you liking the village?' he finally asked.

'It's pretty. But the streets are a bit steep. I don't know how the old people cope.'

'We've got used to it, I suppose. And how about the house? Are you comfortable at your dad's casita?'

Joe nodded. 'It's fine, thanks. So did you see much

of him, while he was here? Did you see him before Christmas?'

Dr Stone glanced at the ceiling. 'Let's see. We had a drink towards the end of the year. November, maybe.'

'Did he appear all right to you?'

'All right? In what way?'

'I mean, did he seem like there was anything bothering him?'

Dr Stone's expression was unreadable. 'Not that I can recollect.'

'Did he ever talk about his business here?'

'Once or twice. Not in great detail.'

'Do you know any of Dad's colleagues?'

'I'm sorry, but I don't. Are you looking for anyone in particular?'

'Did he ever mention a woman called Beatriz?'

Rose appeared to be holding her breath.

'I've heard him mention her,' Dr Stone said. 'But I've never met her.' He continued to smile. Joe looked at Rose. Something was off-kilter.

'Do you know where she lives? I'm trying to find her.'

'Sorry. I haven't the foggiest.'

'Did CJ have any other friends here?'

'I'm not sure. He may have done. As I said, we weren't really that close.'

'You're not in the same business, then?'

'No. I work in Gibraltar. Online gambling.' Dr Stone took a quick gulp of coffee and glanced at his watch. He appeared to be struggling to remain polite.

'So you used to be a doctor?'

'PhD, not MD. Everyone assumes.'

The street cleaner entered the room and whispered something in Dr Stone's ear. Rose, Joe realised, was being incredibly quiet. The way she kept staring at him was unnerving; biting her lower lip; blinking rapidly. The jazz that was playing in the background stopped.

'The man who just left,' Joe said. 'It's strange, I thought I saw him sweeping the streets yesterday.'

Rose smiled and then laughed, a high, nervous giggle. 'No,' she said. 'That was his twin brother. There was only one set of brains to go around that womb.'

Dr Stone turned to Joe.

'Do you speak any Spanish?' he asked.

'I'm trying.'

'Aren't we all,' Rose replied.

She adjusted her vest. Joe spotted a small tattoo on her arm, of a boat. It looked familiar.

'You'll find the language around here particularly difficult to understand,' Dr Stone said. 'They speak the equivalent of a Yorkshire dialect. Dropping words. A nightmare if you're trying to learn.'

Husband and wife exchanged looks and then Dr Stone clapped his hands together and said, 'I'm afraid I've got a bit of work to get back to at the main house.'

Joe stood up.

'No, no – stay. Rose, why don't you show Joe around the place?' Dr Stone took Joe's hand. 'It's been a pleasure meeting you, Joe. Come and visit any time. And again, my condolences.' He nodded at Rose and left. In his absence, the dimensions of the room seemed to expand back to their normal size.

Joe smiled awkwardly at Rose. She smiled back.

'Your tattoo,' Joe pointed. 'What is it, if you don't mind my asking?'

Rose frowned, twisting her arm to look at it. 'It's a Phoenician boat.' She ran her index finger over it.

'I've seen it somewhere before,' he said.

'It's the town emblem; you'll have seen it everywhere. It's from a cave painting high in the mountains. It proves the Straits were much wider back then, that the people of the time were trading between here and Africa. Pretty special, no?'

'Certainly is.'

'Robert doesn't approve. He hit the roof when he saw it. Said I'm too old. But I've always wanted one.'

'Where are you from in England?' he asked. 'I can't place your accent.'

She paused, rubbing her neck. 'We live here more or less full-time. It's not ideal, of course, what with all the hills. But it's beautiful. Have you walked through the canyon?'

Joe shook his head. 'I haven't really been anywhere yet.'

'Oh, you must. It's beautiful at this time of year. And quiet, too. It's the largest cork forest in the world, you know.' There was something bathetic about the assertion, like claiming it was the world's largest sock factory, or the location of the world's longest known sneeze.

He followed her along the corridor. The villa was fitted with all the latest mod cons, specifically designed to accommodate her chair. Ramps led into spacious rooms with vaulted ceilings, rooms packed with bulky furniture and *objets d'art*. They moved into a living room where she stopped and pressed a button on her chair arm. The French windows opened.

'The *pièce de résistance*,' she said, wheeling herself outside.

The cicadas were going crazy. He stared around the blackness, wondering what he was meant to be looking at when a light illuminated a large swimming pool from within. It was steaming.

'Very nice,' he said.

'It's set to a constant twenty-eight degrees. I hate being cold. And we have tons of lilies and datura all around it. I designed the garden.' The aquamarine light reflected in her eyes. 'Helps me maintain muscle tone.'

She rubbed her arms. 'It's chilly. Let's go back in.'

Once inside she wheeled without stopping to the front door. 'Well, it's been nice meeting you, Joe.' She handed him a slip of paper. There was a telephone number scrawled on it. 'That's my number.' She looked down. 'If there's anything you need, anything at all, you know how to reach me.'

It RAINED that night, torrential rain that turned the steep cobbled streets into rivers. Rain that brought the smell of ozone, pine and eucalypt through the open windows.

Almost midnight. The silence of his iPhone turned the room cold. Someone kept phoning and then hanging up. It rang again. Number withheld.

Joe snatched it up. 'Who is this?' Silence. 'Who is this?'

'So have they found your father's body yet?' A man's voice, slurred.

'What are you talking about? Who are you?'

'There was no need to come to Spain.' A posh, southern accent, full of contempt. 'Who put you up to it? Was it Bill? It certainly wasn't Eileen.'

Instinctively, Joe looked around the apartment, and then walked over to the window, expecting to see someone standing in a doorway below, sheltered from the rain, watching the casita.

'I said who is this?'

The man laughed, a vicious jingle. He said, 'I hear you've been showing photographs of CJ around town.'

Joe waited. 'So?'

The man's tone changed. 'Forget it, Joe. I'd be on the next plane back to England if I were you.'

Something about the voice sounded familiar. Joe hesitated. 'Dr Stone?'

The man sighed. 'No.'

'So who are you?'

Joe listened to the slow breathing down the line.

'Lawrence,' he said.

Silence.

'CJ never spoke about me, then?'

'I've never heard of you,' Joe said.

'Yeah right.' There was a click. Joe listened to the dead tone for a long time. He scrolled through the contacts list. Bill. Eileen. He paused. Rose.

He pressed her number and listened to it ring for a long time. He was about to hang up when she answered.

'It's Joe. I hope you don't mind me calling so late?'

Rose cleared her throat. 'What's wrong?'

'I've just had a weird call from someone. He knew that I was here.'

'Who?'

'I thought it was your husband at first.'

'Robert has been in bed for a while now. He's an early riser.'

'Did you ever hear my dad mention someone called Lawrence?' Static crackled down the line. 'Hello?'

'Sorry, I'm still here. No. I've never heard of him.'

Joe sighed and cast his eyes around the room.

'Listen,' she said, 'are you doing anything tomorrow night?'

'I was hoping to speak to your husband again.'

'Robert's away tomorrow. In Malaga. Pepe and the rest of the staff are also off work, some religious festival crap. So I thought if you weren't too busy in the evening, we could keep each other company? You can ask me all the questions you like.'

He hung up. Listened to the rain outside.

The following morning, Joe splashed some water onto his face, put some clean clothes on, and walked down into the canyon. He passed large tracts of cacti and two burros in a field, and spooked a pair of wiry dogs who pursued him for a hundred metres, barking.

When he reached the valley bottom, he followed the river along the wooded canyon sides, choked with oleander and eucalypt, though mainly cork oak. Most of the trees were stripped of their bark, their blood-red bodies exposed beneath. Turtles, basking on rocks, plopped into the river whenever he got close, and wherever he stepped there was the smell of herbs crushed underfoot: rosemary, thyme, mint – a reminder of Eileen's herb garden back home.

He walked until he came to the outlet of the stream that had the makings of a sandy beach. It looked familiar. He took out the photograph from Bill's tie drawer and scanned the landscape: the profile of the trees; the camber of the sandbank; the bows of the river. Nothing matched.

The morning sun licked his skin. The occasional butterfly or dragonfly cut across his view. Griffin vultures circled on cushions of air, their screeches echoing through the canyon. He watched the vultures for a long time, admiring the way they climbed so effortlessly, without a single beat of their wings.

His mind was a farrago of conflicting thought. Was he wasting his time out here? Was he looking in the wrong place? Was there even anything to find?

He noticed a minuscule rip in the fabric of the sky: an aeroplane heading north from Africa, its contrail lit white-hot by the sun.

He wished he were on that plane, heading home.

Walking back up the steep streets into town, Eileen phoned.

'How are you getting on?' she asked. 'Any news?'

'Not yet,' he replied. 'Nothing concrete, anyway. But something is up.'

She sighed.

'How about you?' Joe asked. 'Have you heard anything from the police?'

'Slater and one of the other detectives dropped by. They asked where you were. I said you'd gone back down to London, though I don't see why we should lie.'

'Neither do I, Mum, but it's probably a good idea, for now. How's Grandad?'

'I don't know. I'd love to get a peek inside his head. Empty, probably.'

'Don't be horrible, Mum.'

'I'm only messing. Look, I'll call you later. I start back at work this afternoon.'

'Oh. Right.'

'Don't sound like that. I need to do something,' she said. 'And I can't be on compassionate leave forever. I'm going crazy in this house, waiting.'

'Mum . . .' He hesitated. 'Have you ever heard of a guy called Lawrence?'

'No. Why, should I have?'

'It's just a name that cropped up. Don't worry.'

Rabbit stood in Cass's bedroom. Slats of light fell through the blinds, across the room and empty bed. There was a smell of sleep-breath, of cheap perfume bought off the market, and sweaty insoles. Pictures and photographs hung from the wall in a higgledy-piggledy fashion in mismatching frames, a few random postcards Blu-tacked beside them. The room hadn't changed since Rabbit first came to live here, as an angry, grief-stricken ten-year-old. A few daisies sat dying in a vase of stagnant water.

Standing on the landing, she shouted down the stairs again, 'Cass.'

Alone in the house.

It was almost a week since she last spoke to Kate. She knew it was a risk, but if she just turned up at the house, surely it would be more difficult for Kate to ask her to leave, wouldn't it? They had to get beyond this, whatever this was. She checked the clock. Kate would be back from her shift now. Fuck it.

She knocked at the door and stepped back. Kate answered it, looking startled, dressed in a tracksuit.

'Hi,' Rabbit said. 'Where've you been?'

The expression on her face was unreadable. 'Busy,' she said. 'I need to study.'

'Why? You don't start uni until September.'

'I like to be on top of things. Ahead. It's important to me.'

And I'm not, Rabbit thought. 'All work and no play,' she said. 'Come on, let's go for a drive. Just for an hour. You need a break. Wrap up. You won't even have to get out of the car if you don't want to. Or we can just grab a quick pint.'

Kate gave a weary look. 'I'm sorry, Rabbit. I told you, I've things to do. I'd rather you phoned before you came, actually.'

'I've been phoning all week. You never answer.'

Kate sighed. Their eyes locked.

Kate said, 'Look, I'll see you soon, yeah?'

'What about the Crow tomorrow night?'

'I can't, I'm looking after Hannah.'

'I could help.'

Kate folded her arms, sighed again.

Rabbit peered down at her hands and realised they were shaking. Rankled, a caustic taste in her throat, she said, 'OK.'

The front gate clattered behind her and she turned to find herself face to face with Eileen Arms.

Eileen examined Rabbit for a second before looking at Kate.

'Is your mum in?'

Kate shook her head. 'She's out.'

'Oh. Right.'

'Do you want to come in and wait?'

Eileen squinted at Rabbit. 'Don't I know you?' Her splintery voice and tear-pink eyes. She looked sleep-deprived, hungry.

'I don't think so.' Rabbit put her head down. 'See you later,' she muttered, and walked away.

EARLY SUNDAY morning, Rabbit woke to see headlights moving across the ceiling. The two strips of light paused in the centre of her room for a second, and then disappeared. She rose rapidly and dashed to her window and stared out into the blue, silent dawn. A silver car, up near the Social Club. A flare of light: the sulphur head of a match being struck, and then the red end of a cigarette's glow.

She stepped away from the window, crept back over to her bed, and lay there for a long time before she heard the car move away, shifting through gears down the road.

She'd tried calling Kate a few times over the weekend, but all she got back were cursory texts. *Not feeling well. Need to study. See you soon.*

That afternoon, she headed downstairs to find Cass sat in front of the TV.

'Is there any booze?' Rabbit asked.

Cass eyed her steadily. Deep down, Rabbit knew Cass was chuffed she was staying in more often, spending more time with her – not traipsing the streets, as Cass put it.

'If I pour you a drink, you'll still be going in to work tomorrow, right?'

Rabbit sighed. 'My name Lazy Daisy? Just make it strong.'

Cass headed into the kitchen while Rabbit surfed the Sky channels. Heard the sucky sound of the freezer door open and close. Ice tinkling in a glass. Lime being chopped. Cass brought in two G&Ts and they cracked their glasses together.

'Up your bum,' Cass said.

'No babies,' Rabbit replied.

Instantly the air soured. They sat beside each other, sipping in silence. Cass forced a smile out — a smile that was meant to reassure Rabbit that this wasn't a prelude into a lament about him.

Eventually Rabbit said, 'I went to the old house last week.'

Cass leaned over, lifted the remote, and switched off the TV.

'The anniversary?'

Rabbit nodded. 'I went to the cottage, and all these memories started flooding back. Like Mum had this old biscuit tin full of buttons that she kept in a chest of drawers. I'd play with the buttons for hours, making patterns of numbers. I remembered her helping me cover my school-books with wallpaper. Remember we used to do that?'

Cass smiled.

'And she would order me orange juice in a milk bottle from the milkman every Friday, as a treat. It always tasted better from a glass bottle.'

Rabbit noticed the cracks of Cass's mouth, filled with grainy lipstick. She had been to the Bingo that afternoon. She rarely wore make-up.

'I remember everything after that point,' Rabbit looked up, 'but before then my memory is just blurred.'

Cass sighed long and deep.

'I saw Eileen Arms yesterday.'

Cass sniffed. 'Don't you think it's all a bit strange?'

'What is?'

'That he's missing? Personally, I think it's an insurance job. I always thought there was something dodgy about him.'

Rabbit sat in silence. She wondered whether Kate was suspicious about the way she reacted when Eileen appeared, whether she'd seen anything.

CJ Arms in his watery grave. Maybe it's better to think it's an accident. She remembered reading an article about eyewitness testimonies being unreliable. Credibility. Inaccuracies in their accounts. Remembering erroneous events that didn't actually occur. But she knew what she saw, and she was protecting the Arms family from the truth.

She almost believed it.

IT WAS like a normal evening, like two new friends enjoying each other's company. Except it wasn't. Rose wheeled herself over to the stereo and changed the music.

'It's so hot in here,' she said. 'Shall we go for a swim? Or there's the hot tub? It's lovely and cool.'

Joe shrugged. 'I'm all right.'

'Oh, go on. Why not? You're not shy, are you? A body like that. Come on, indulge an old lady.'

Joe smiled, mulling it over. 'I've got no trunks.'

She laughed. 'I'd lend you some of Robert's, but I doubt they would fit. Just wear your undies. Or you can always borrow one of my swimming costumes?'

'I'll manage, thanks.'

She grinned mischievously. 'Take the bottle. See you out there.'

Ten minutes later, he was bubbling in the tub, his head tilted back, staring at the stars. He heard the screen door sliding. Rose wheeled herself out, hair tied up. She was wearing a skimpy white bikini.

'I can either get the hoist,' she said, 'or you can be a gentleman and give me a lift.'

She examined him while he climbed out, a smirk on her face. He lifted her out of the chair, her skin cold against his body – and slowly walked back into the tub. She pushed herself to one side and sat facing him, exchanging glances through the steam. The roll, burble and splash of water. He peered out into the surrounding darkness where cicadas romanced.

She broke the silence. 'Drinks, Jeeves.'

He filled her glass. She sat back and sighed, pulling a small joint from her hair. He thought about the tin of weed secreted in the cupboard in the casita. The light from within the tub cast patterns over her shoulders and neck, dapples of light that made her green eyes sparkle. He tried not to look at her breasts but the water slicked her skin, turning her bikini slightly see-through. Did she know? Of course she knew. There was a static in the air, a sexual agitation. Just keep looking into her eyes, he told himself. Those gorgeous green eyes.

'You're in pretty good shape,' she said.

He shrugged. 'I haven't been to the gym in ages.'

'You don't seem vain, though,' she said.

'I hope not.'

'No, what I mean is, I always assumed men who spent so much time in the gym also spent a lot of time looking at themselves in the mirror. More than is healthy.'

He shrugged again.

She squinted at him. 'You've no idea, have you?'

'I don't particularly like what I see in the mirror,' he said. 'I got picked on. I guess when I look in the mirror I still see that kid, somehow.'

She shook her head.

He could feel the night air blowing across his face and shoulders, thrilling at his neck. He tried to relax, but his mind drifted back to CJ, to Dr Stone, to Lawrence.

She exhaled smoke and passed him the joint. He stared at it, unsure, then took a drag and passed it back, struggling not to cough.

'I'm sorry to have called last night,' he said. 'I'm just not sure what I'm supposed to be doing. Did you ask Robert, you know . . . if he knows someone called Lawrence?'

She shook her head. 'Sorry. No.' She blinked at him a few times. 'You've never explained what you do for a living.'

Play along. Pretty soon, she might let something slip.

He said, 'I remember my parents sat me down and asked me what I was planning to do. It was the day I got my GCSE exam results. I said I wanted to work for a year at the local ice-cream factory, to save up enough money to go travelling. Dad said, Well, you'll have to start paying us rent then, and put money towards food and bills. A third all the way. I laughed. I mean, I'd only just turned sixteen. But they just kept staring at me. I honestly thought they were joking.'

Rose blinked at him, forlorn.

'But now I can see that he did it out of love,' he said. 'No one in the family had been to university before. They were pinning all their hopes on me. But for a few years I resented them. I just didn't understand anything at that time. I thought I knew it all.'

'And you knew *nada*.'

'Exactly. Not that I'm claiming to know that much now.'

He stared at the boat tattoo on her arm as she put the

joint to her mouth. She took a final hit, flicked the joint into the darkness, and cleared her throat.

Silence.

'So have you travelled much?' she asked.

'Not as much as I'd like. I hope to do a lot more.'

'Where's your favourite place?'

'I don't know.'

'Other than being in this hot tub with me? Come on.'

'I love America,' he said. 'We used to go to New York now and then. Coney Island. Pat Auletta Pier with all those plastic palm trees everywhere, and fat, oiled-up Sicilians wearing Speedos and comedy sunglasses, sunbathing on benches. I used to like watching the bikers going up and down the esplanade on their Harleys.'

'Ha. The seedy seaside. Sounds like Hastings used to be.'

'You know Hastings?'

The atmosphere, the scene, dissolved like melting celluloid. She blinked at him.

'Why did you mention Hastings?'

She looked away from him. 'No reason. I've just visited once or twice.'

'That's funny,' he said. 'Dad used to live there.'

She continued to stare out into the darkness of the garden, the pulse in her neck fluttering. The silence lasted a solid thirty seconds.

'You knew him from back then, didn't you?' As he said it, he felt a catch in his chest. He opened his mouth, trying to form the words, but they wouldn't come. 'I think you should tell me what you know,' he said.

She glared at him and then grabbed his hand, yanked it under the water, and placed it on her breast.

He pulled his hand away.

'What's wrong?' she said.

'What are you hiding?' He stood up, shaking his head. 'This was a bad idea. I should go.' He offered her his hand. 'Do you want help getting out?'

She turned away. 'I can manage.'

He kept looking down at her but she wouldn't meet his eyes.

'Sorry,' he said, and stepped out.

'You're looking in the wrong place.'

She said it so quietly he thought he'd imagined it. 'What?'

She pushed the hair back from her face. Her mascara had started to run. 'Beatriz,' she said. 'She's in Puerto Sotogrande. On your dad's yacht.' She blinked up at him. 'Now get out.'

HE APPROACHED the casita in the darkness. There was a car parked outside. As he stepped into the side passage, he could hear something. Music. The smell of cigarettes. The door was open. Two men were sitting on his couch. They exchanged glances. One looked big, the other pencil-thin. They were both dark-skinned and had long, curly blue-black hair. Gypsies.

The big one stood up. 'Joseph. I am Raúl, this Paquito.'

Joe stared. 'You've broken into my house.' He tried to keep the alarm out of his voice. 'Get out, before I call the police.' He turned to the thin man. 'Now.'

'He *habla* no English.'

Raúl pointed at the chair. 'Sit.' Then he pointed at the table. There was a line of white powder, a near-empty bottle of whiskey, a jug of water and ice.

Joe raised a hand. 'How do you know my name?'

Raúl jabbed a finger at the line. 'Take.' He grabbed Joe around the neck and pushed his head towards the table. Joe felt something release deep within his brain: the flight or fight reflex. He spun round, batting Raúl's hand away with force.

'Get the fuck out.'

The two men started talking in a fast, lilting jabber, shouting at each other and gesticulating, arguing with smiles on their faces, or maybe not arguing at all.

'Did you know CJ?' Joe asked.

Raúl stood before him, opened his arms, and began to sing. Machine-gun clapping and slightly out-of-key singing, like a fucked-up version of the blues. Flamenco. He put so much emphasis into every tortured syllable, every venomous oath with his cocaine-raw voice, that it made Joe smile and when he smiled, they both slapped him around the shoulders and squeezed his muscles, sizing him up. He knew he could take them both, if he had to.

'What do you want?' Joe shouted, silencing him.

Raúl looked emotionally wrecked. Paquito said something under his breath and Raúl sat down, drifting by degrees into a stupor.

They both stared at him. Animal stares. Sweating, breathing hard. Then Paquito started to weep. Sitting in a chair on the opposite side of the room, he rubbed his face, sobbing like a child. Raúl laid a hand across his heart and made a fist, pounding his chest, '*Corazón, corazón, corazón . . .*'

Paquito squinted at Joe, dragging his thumb across his neck.

Joe blinked, waiting for him to do it again.

Paquito got to his feet and stood beside Raúl. They reached around their backs simultaneously. Knives.

'Our sister,' Raúl said. 'Beatriz.'

The pulse knocked through Joe's veins, breathing shallow, hands clammy. Instantly he knew he was about to be killed and that the vultures he loved watching would soon be picking his corpse clean in the mountains.

'Beatriz. Your father. Gone. Where?'

Feet wide apart, gaze fixed on their knees, Joe waited for a lunge. He flexed his muscles in turn because the adrenalin was making them seize. He clenched and unclenched his fists and then he met their eyes, filled with wet sadness.

'I don't know,' Joe said.

'Liar.' Raúl rubbed his fingers together. '*Comprar*. You *comprar*. *¿Quieres comprarla?*'

Spines bent, cupping the knives in their hands, their shadows grabbed Joe's shadow by the throat and squeezed. Time dissolved. Joe's head throbbed. He stepped backwards, out of reach.

'My father is missing,' Joe said. 'Check the fucking Internet if you don't believe me. He crashed into a lake. Drowned.'

They looked at each other, expressionless. Raúl started to sing again and Paquito slapped Raúl in the chest, making him stop.

The three men breathed into the silence.

Joe said, 'And I don't know where Beatriz is. That's the truth.' He pointed towards the door. 'Just get the fuck out.'

Raúl held his knife out, tip pointing upwards.

'Ask Rose or Dr Stone,' Joe said. 'They know.'

The two Gypsies laughed.

'I don't know anything,' Joe shouted. '*Nada*.'

The two men studied him for a while, and then nodded. Raúl reached for his mobile. He pressed a number and held the phone to his ear. 'Lawrence,' he said, and then muttered a few words in Spanish and hung up.

Joe put his ear against the back of the casita door and listened to the sound of their car starting and moving off. He packed what remained of his things. Morning light was slatting through the blinds and the dogs and burros had started their manic dawn serenade in the streets outside. He remembered his MacBook and was surprised to find it still sitting in the cupboard drawer.

He checked Google Earth and found a small marina called Puerto Sotogrande about fifty kilometres south-east from Jimena, in a small coastal town called Torreguadiaro.

He grabbed his bag, and locked the casita door behind him.

THAT SATURDAY evening, Frankie took Rabbit to the Crow. Kate was in the corner with a couple of other part-timers from the factory.

The music was loud. Rabbit drank quickly. 'Come and dance!' Frankie stood and beckoned to her. There was Kate, right behind him. He threw his arms up and turned round. Rabbit watched Kate and Frankie dance. Kate was flirting with him, no doubt about it. Rubbing Rabbit's face in it. Rabbit looked at her anew; she didn't know how to read the situation. She hadn't seen Kate at work at all that week; she suspected Kate had asked to clean in a different part of the factory. Frankie danced with his hands in his pockets, doing his funny shuffle, as if he were too cool to let himself go, oblivious to what Kate was doing. Kate's graceful boogie, shaking her long curly hair in the flashing disco lights. People were watching, thinking they were seeing the beginning of something.

Rabbit necked her drink, went to the bar and ordered herself another house double. When she looked back at them again, things had changed, shifted. Another girl was on the dance floor. Frankie grabbed her arm, and Kate lost her dancing partner.

Later, Rabbit and Kate were sitting in Rabbit's car at the back of the Crow. They could hear music from the jukebox inside the pub and see into the beer garden where Frankie had his tongue down the girl's throat.

'How sweet,' Kate said. 'Young love.'

Rabbit reached across and held Kate's hand. Kate looked at her curiously.

'You've been avoiding me at work,' Rabbit said.

'Look, my head's been all over the place.'

'Mine too. So what's happening?'

Kate shrugged.

'I only get to see you every two weeks, is that it? And the rest of the time you avoid me. I can't be doing with one-offs. What's going on?'

'I don't bloody know.'

After a moment, Rabbit asked, 'Do you fancy a drive?'

'You sure you haven't had too much to drink?'

'I'm OK,' Rabbit lied. 'I've been on lemonade most of the night.'

'Actually, we could go back to mine,' Kate said. 'I've got the place to myself. Hannah and Mum are away until tomorrow night.'

Rabbit kept turning the water hotter. Kate's hair was so slick, so dark, as the shower water poured over them both. The mirror of Kate's body in her hands, hands unlocking muscles, opening each other up.

About 4 a.m., Kate woke Rabbit and asked her if she

wanted to stay or go home. Rabbit stared at Kate's face in the demi-light. Her lips were swollen and her breath smelled of gin and smoke, of Nina Ricci and juniper.

Rabbit said, 'There's something I need to tell you.'

Kate waited. 'What?'

Rabbit opened her mouth, but she couldn't say the words. I'm the anonymous caller. Curling a hand around Kate's neck, she brought her down onto her again.

When she left that morning, Rabbit said, 'So I guess I'll see you in two weeks.'

'No,' Kate said. 'Come round later. Please.'

They saw each other every night that week, driving away from the factory to the same country lane, a secluded dirt track five miles out of town. Surrounded on all sides by tall pine trees, they eased themselves onto the back seat, fitting themselves into one another within the tight confines of Rabbit's car, engine running, heater on full blast.

The strength of Kate's desire shocked Rabbit, and there was nothing she wouldn't do in that moment – moments when nothing else existed; no fear; no stress; no CJ Arms or Joe and Eileen; no man at the lake – and Rabbit was compelled to follow Kate's lust to its source, that hard, painful kernel of longing.

They'd rest for a while, skinning up by the dashboard light, the windows fogged. Five nights of body angles on the back seat, hands and knees and repositioning. No part of their bodies left untouched, ignored, nerve ends and synapses firing in the dark interior, wanting to follow their fingers and tongues in there.

On the fifth night, Kate said, 'I really fancy a drink.'

'It's late opening at the Crow,' Rabbit said.

'Let's go.'

Kate touched Rabbit's hand and they shared a private smile. The pub was busy. The band had just finished and New Order's 'Blue Monday' was playing on the jukebox. Rabbit found herself switching off.

There had been times over the past five days when she'd almost told Kate she loved her. And there had been times when she almost told Kate her secret.

She scanned the people in the pub and recalled the feeling she'd been having lately, of being watched, observed. The panic began – a steady pulse at the back of her mind.

She did a double take of a man sitting at the end of the bar on the opposite side of the room. His eyes combing the room, alighting on a table next to Rabbit's. Eyes radiating cold, hard heat.

Him.

She put her head down and shuffled her bum along the seat until Kate's head was obscuring her.

The fear was all-consuming.

Kate stopped talking. 'Are you all right?'

'Do you mind if we leave?'

'You've got a whole drink left.'

'I think I've had enough.'

She leaned over a little and saw the man standing up from his stool and saying something to the barmaid. He turned and headed towards the Gents.

Rabbit grabbed her coat. 'I'll see you outside.'

GROGAN WAS parked outside the Arms house when he saw the Honda Civic again. She pulled up along the street. Honked her horn.

The Weir girl walked out, climbed into the car, leaned across and gave her a kiss.

Grogan put his car into gear, followed.

They drove out of town. The thrum of a cattle grid beneath his tyres as they hit the moor. They pulled into a secluded lane, hit the lights.

Grogan parked nearby and walked across the field until he was forty feet away. Standing beside a pine tree with his binoculars, he glassed the two of them through the rear window. The red end of a cigarette or joint being shared. Their faces lit in the soft green shadows of the dashboard lights. Dull laughter. They climbed between the front seats, onto the back. Watched them fit themselves into one another until the back window fogged, opaque, green-tinged.

Later, he tailed them back to Ravenstor. The woman driving dropped the Weir girl off, and then Grogan followed the driver as she made her way back onto Nether Tor. She parked directly below the Social Club. With his binoculars, he watched her climb from her car, lock the door, and then walk beneath the privet arch over the front gate.

Same house. Same girl.

He made the call.

Week Five

The taxi drove south-east, down through the foothills towards the coast, passing through uninspiring, dusty countryside, and along a near-empty motorway for twenty miles or so. They stopped at a petrol station, filled up the tank and then the driver had a smoke while chatting on his mobile.

Joe mulled over what he knew – or rather, didn't know. So Beatriz was a Gypsy. But how was CJ connected to them, and what was Lawrence's role in all of this? What was CJ up to out here? And why were Robert and Rose pretending they didn't know Beatriz when they obviously did? And what did Rose mean when she said 'CJ's yacht'? CJ didn't own a yacht; she must be mistaken. What if Beatriz wasn't out here – what if it was some kind of trap?

They pulled up outside a marina, next to what looked like a security cabin.

The driver pointed. 'In there.'

Joe walked into the smoke-filled room and showed the photograph of Beatriz to the security guard, and explained why he was there. The guard nodded and asked for his passport and then went into another room and made a couple of calls. After a few minutes, the guard came back, and beckoned Joe to follow him. They walked through the security cabin and along the pontoons. Joe could make out the shape of a gun clipped to the man's hip. The guard turned, gave Joe his passport back and pointed out a yacht.

'Gracias,' Joe said, and watched the guard walk away before stepping into the cockpit. He knocked on the cabin roof though the door was wide open.

'Hello?'

He was surprised by the amount of space and headroom below. The galley was all cherry veneer and granite work-tops with bar-style seating and cream carpets. There was a stowaway table and buckskin sleeper sofa, and a digital home theatre system with cube Bose speakers. There were two sleeper cabins, both with double beds.

Was this really his dad's?

He looked in her room, the pillowcase grubby with make-up, a pink T-shirt crumpled on the bed. Drawers had puked their innards of blouses and skirts, knickers and bras. More make-up scattered across the kitchen table. A small, circular hand mirror, finger-smudged. A hairbrush spun with blue-black hair.

Back in the cockpit, he sat on the cream leather seats, listening to the sound of water glutting against the hull. He ran through the imagined conflict he would have when she finally appeared. He would play the part of the clueless son, she the waiflike ingénue.

He heard clomps along the pontoon. She climbed over the gunwale into the cockpit. She was extraordinary-looking, even more so than in the photograph, but her beautiful eyes were black holes that filled him with a sense of vertigo.

'What?' she asked. She was swaying but the yacht wasn't moving. Drunk. 'What are you doing here?'

'Rose told me . . .'

She smiled, nodded. 'You look so much like him,' she said.

'I've been at Dad's casita,' he said. 'I had a visit from your brothers last night.'

Beatriz just grimaced. 'I'm exhausted. Can we talk later? You can take the other cabin if you need to sleep.'

Her accent, her idiom, was almost upper class – crisp, clipped sentences, with only a trace of a Spanish accent.

'I'd rather we talk first.'

She growled, 'Later, OK,' and headed down the steps, banging into the door and cursing in Spanish. In the silence that followed, he could hear her yawning, and then the slam of her cabin door.

He stared out across the waves into the citrus light. He felt both edgy and sluggish, his mind full of conflicting impulses.

His iPhone trilled.

'I don't think those boys had very nice plans for you, did they?'

Lawrence.

'A thank-you would be polite,' he added.

'Whatever.'

'So I hear you left already? In a bit of a rush, by all accounts.'

'. . .'

'Oh, I sent Eileen a birthday card.'

Her first birthday without CJ in thirty-seven years. Joe had completely forgotten.

'You leave her out of this,' Joe said.

'Or what, you'll go to the police? Do you not think they'll be wondering what you're doing over there?' *There*. So he wasn't in Spain. 'Your father's not squeaky clean, you know.'

'No. I don't know. Everyone seems to know more than I do.'

'Well, I'll tell you. Your father was a greedy bastard. He owes me money.'

'That's a lie. He doesn't owe you anything. He's a good man.'

Lawrence chuckled. 'I've looked into you, Joe. I know who you are. What you've been up to. How about you spot your old man, seeing as you're not short of a few pounds? That's if he doesn't appear first.'

He hung up. Seconds later, his phone rang again. Eileen.

'Sorry I missed you yesterday,' he said, trying to shake the tension from his voice.

She cut him off. 'Have you found her then?'

'I'm with her now. I've not had a chance to talk to her though. Not properly.'

'Why you whispering?'

'I don't know.'

'Is she pretty?'

'Don't, Mum.'

She fell silent.

'Mum?'

'But can you talk?'

'Just for a minute.'

Down the line, he heard a door open and close, footsteps,

another door open and close, and he could picture exactly where she was, in the kitsch downstairs toilet with its doily loo-roll holder and tang of pine cleaner.

She said Bill had fallen at the allotment and hurt his leg. She sounded flat, distant.

'Nothing serious, duck, don't fret. But he's in a right tither.' She sighed. 'It's started again. His hoarding.'

'It's worse?'

'He keeps going through the recycling bins. No one in the street is safe, especially on bin day. He's out there rooting through the bags. He found a stack of catalogues from somewhere. It's embarrassing, Joe. I wish you were here.'

'You should speak to the doctor again.'

She breathed down the line. 'I had a walk up to the cemetery yesterday,' she said. 'Don't ask me why. I went to the new part on the hilltop where the memorial stones are, you know? I thought it would be nice to put something for CJ up there.'

'It's only been five weeks, Mum . . .' He heard a noise coming from below. 'I'll call you later. Have a nice birthday. Love you.'

He stared at the screen, picturing her listening to the dial tone and wondering what he was getting up to. England seemed like a distant dream. The lakeside town, the house overlooking the valley, snowy and black and white. A noir world CJ inhabited.

He went down into the cabin and opened his MacBook, ordered Eileen a bouquet of flowers, and lay down to wait.

MEDITERRANEAN LIGHT muscled its way through the narrow hatch and onto the cabin wall. Joe could smell tobacco and eggs. From the galley kitchen above, he could hear Beatriz singing along to the radio. He'd slept the night away.

Beatriz had tidied up the place and was making them sandwiches: *bocadillos* filled with fried chorizo, cheese and slices of tomato. She put the pan down and smiled at him. They ate in silence. He was starving. The morning light reflected off the water, throwing spangles across her skin. Whenever another boat drove by, the yacht wobbled in its wake and the ropes and lanyards around them plinked and clunked. The wet sounds made him perceive the world differently; the place, the situation, was alive to his senses.

She picked up a packet of tobacco. He observed her as she rolled a cigarette – an unconscious, automatic act. Her fingernails were bitten to the quick.

'Help yourself,' she said, pushing the tobacco towards him.

'Thanks, but I don't smoke.'

He looked around the cockpit at the mysterious instrumentation.

'Why are you here, Beatriz?'

She shrugged.

'Who are you? How do you know my dad?'

She turned her head and blew out a thin stream of smoke. 'You know who I am.'

'I know your name. And I now know your brothers. They came to see me at Dad's casita.'

'You said. And I'm sorry about that.'

'They're after you, you know. They were after me too, but Lawrence spoke to them and they left.'

'You've spoken to Lawrence?'

'He's phoned me a few times. Scumbag.'

She squinted at him. 'Do you know him?'

'I'd never heard of him until I came here. I don't know what he wants, but he's keeping tabs on me. He knows where I am. He must know something about Dad.'

She shook her head.

'So where is he? Lawrence, I mean.'

'At sea. On his yacht. Where no one can find him, I guess.'

She chewed on her thumb and squinted at him with a look resembling pity. 'Don't worry about my brothers,' she said. 'Believe me, if they wanted to kill you, you wouldn't be sat here right now.'

'And that's meant to make me feel better, is it? What does *comprar* mean?'

She snorted. 'My brother is the Gypsy king of Castellar. They'll want you to buy me from them. For their loss of earnings. Because CJ shut the operation down.'

'I don't understand.'

'You really have no idea what CJ was up to out here?'

'No. I told you. That's what I came here to find out.'

'When I heard Jesse was gone . . .'

Joe had never heard anyone refer to CJ by his middle name before.

'Everyone got him wrong,' she said. 'My brothers. They think Jesse shut the business down because of me.'

'IFX?'

'Uh-huh. They think we were having an affair, and that I influenced him. It's all about money with them. But Jesse, he was just a very sweet man. I've known him all my life. Since I was a little girl.'

Every remark she made seemed to have a depth to it, another level of inference. Scribbled notes in the margins, whisperings just out of earshot. He stared at her, looking for clues that would give her away, reveal the truth.

'What have your brothers got to do with my dad?'

She sighed, got to her feet and disappeared below. Two minutes later, she reappeared wearing a black swimming costume. She nodded at him.

'I always swim in the morning. I can't think straight without it. If you want to talk you better come along.' She pointed. 'That island, you think you can make it?'

Out at sea, he noticed the horizon was dotted with the black rectangles of dredgers, about a dozen of them. He spotted the small island, about forty metres from the shore further down the coast.

Nodded.

They swam past the end of the jetty where the water became cooler. He felt his lungs tighten. She was a strong swimmer and he couldn't match her pace. After five minutes or so, he stopped and looked back towards the port, at the garishly painted, pastiche architecture, the newly planted palm trees and the dark mountains behind, dotted with *pueblos* and summer mansions. The marina was a forest of masts and sails. Hotel shutters offered their blank gazes and a breeze carried the sound of mopeds from the esplanade.

He swam on, slowly. As he reached the shore, Beatriz was sitting, squeezing water from her hair.

The island was just a few jaggedy rocks with scant vegetation and a couple of desperate-looking trees, but there was a beach all around it, the sand pristine, almost white. Completely empty, they had the place to themselves.

It was difficult not to look at her as she reclined on the sand; it was the pose from the photograph. In fact, he was sure this was the exact same spot the photograph had been taken. Beatriz liked to be looked at and he liked looking.

He sat on the sand next to her.

'I know what you're thinking,' she said, 'but nothing happened between me and Jesse. Sorry if I upset your mother when I called. I really liked him. Over the past few years, we became really close. Good friends. That's all.'

'You never slept with him?'

She threw him a dirty look. 'Of course not, *cabrón*. He's older than my father.'

'Why did you say you were scared your brothers will find you? They can find you here, surely?'

She laughed. 'They're illiterate dogs. They can barely tie their own shoelaces. And do you not think the security needs to be good with all of these million-euro yachts floating around?'

'What would they do to you if you went home? And what have they got to do with my dad?'

'You're a terrible detective, do you know that?'

'And what's the story with Lawrence?'

A smile touched the corners of her mouth. 'Him.'

'Why is he phoning me? He mentioned debts.'

'He thinks Jesse is still alive, apparently.'

'Who told you that?'

'Rose,' she said.

'So she knows Lawrence?'

She nodded. 'He thinks Jesse will turn up here. We're both part of a game of cat and mouse in Lawrence's head.'

'That's stupid.'

She muttered something in Spanish, and then asked, 'Why do you think he sent my brothers to see you last night?'

'I've no idea.'

'Every man's reach exceeds his grasp,' she said. 'Lawrence and Robert are brothers.'

'Really?'

'Jesse met them in a nightclub when he was seventeen or eighteen. It was Lawrence's club in Hastings.'

'You know about Hastings?'

'Are you going to keep interrupting me?'

'Sorry.'

'There was some trouble, a fight in the club. Jesse got involved. Stepped in. That's where he got the scar. The one on his neck.'

She paused, watching him.

'He told me that he got that scar coming off a motor-bike,' Joe said, shaking his head. 'He never mentioned anything about a nightclub.'

'Lawrence said he was impressed. They became friends. Associates.'

Just then a small yacht appeared, very close to the island, with three men on board. It was so close Joe could hear the music playing on their stereo. Beatriz raised her hand to shield her eyes from the sun and matched the men's gaze.

He looked at her again. The scar. Hastings. The debts. It wasn't possible, was it? And what if CJ had escaped the crash at the lake? No. He wouldn't do that to them.

As if privy to his thoughts, she said, 'Believe what you want, but it's true.'

'It was my grandfather Bill who suggested I come out here to find you, to find out what went on towards the end of last year. Dad wasn't himself. But I guess you know that? He thinks something happened to Dad out here, and from the little you've told me, I'm sure he's right.'

She appeared lost in thought.

'All I'm interested in is finding him, Beatriz. Getting to the bottom of the accident,' he said, 'and what happened out here.'

'You really have no idea what Jesse was up to?'

'No. I told you. That's what I came here to find out. I know nothing. None of us do. If you liked him so much, then I think he'd want us to know.'

She eyed him curiously.

'What the fuck have your brothers got to do with my dad?'

'I'm sorry.'

'What for?'

She sighed. 'That it's me telling you this. My brothers, they collect it off the beaches at Tarifa. It comes over on the boats straight from Morocco. Tangiers.'

Joe thought about the Super 8 film, the random images of Morocco. It could have been Tangiers. 'When you say "it", what do you mean?' he asked.

'Coke.'

She measured his reaction.

He laughed. 'Cocaine?'

'Uh-huh.'

'You're joking.'

'No. The cash used to come to IFX to be converted into fifty-euro notes. Fifties, because they're easy to conceal. Then the coke makes its way up through Europe and lands on a beach somewhere . . .'

'Dad was involved in cocaine?'

She tutted. 'Kent, I think it was. Somewhere near a nuclear power station.'

'In Kent?'

'It gets cut up in London and then cars pick it up at service stations and it goes out into the country like that.' She spread the fingers on both of her hands, emphasising the point. 'Bang. Like a virus.'

He didn't know how to navigate the information. There was something tale-mongerish about her tone, but after the past forty-eight hours, he knew, deep down, that what she was telling him must be true.

She said, 'They used these pay-as-you-go mobiles all the time. They were scared of being bugged, of surveillance by the Metropolitan Police. The Sisters, Jesse called them.'

'What sisters?'

'Special Intelligence Section. SIS.'

'You're telling me Dad was in on all of this?'

She blinked at him. 'It's complicated.'

'Go on.'

'I had to piece it all together over the years. No one wanted me involved. *Implicación*. I used to listen in on them talking, pretending I wasn't interested. I grew up knowing what my brothers were involved in. That's no secret, everyone knows that. But the money-laundering side – well, that was different. Jesse made the illicit licit.'

She leaned towards him and he could smell the tobacco on her breath. She narrowed her eyes, her thick lips moved, mouthing his thoughts. She was beginning to consume him.

'Jesse was the main cashier. When he shut things down, it had a domino effect, right down the supply line. The smuggling route was broken, leaving my brothers and the Moroccan guys seriously pissed off. They were also smuggling cash. One of the banks here was in on it, don't ask me which. They were blending funds. Purchasing assets.'

'The yacht? It's Dad's?'

She nodded. 'Jesse kept copies of all of their financial transactions from before the euro came in. That's when they made most of their money. Jesse used the two-year run-up to the euro to gather as much cash as he could. He placed it all in a bank somewhere and it was all converted the day the euro came in. All this cash was now legitimate. Mobile across the EU. But Jesse kept the records. He created a paper trail leading right to Lawrence. Insurance against anything bad happening. There was no way he could just say he'd had enough, that he wanted out, to retire and walk away. Gangsters don't retire. It's the only way he could close the company without, you know. Without reprisals. It was his safety net. He was desperate to get out. You see, Lawrence reaped all of the benefits.'

'So this is why Dad was scared last year? Because he knew Lawrence would come after him?'

She looked mournful. 'I'm not sure.'

'Has this got anything to do with the crash?'

She shrugged. 'Lawrence doesn't know what Jesse has done with the paperwork. Think about it. The last thing he wants is for something bad to happen to Jesse. That's why he's been calling you. He's nervous.' She paused. 'But what do I know?'

'Did you notice any change in Dad, the last time you saw him?'

'I did see him upset one time. I found him sitting in the dark crying. He was really drunk. But he wouldn't talk to me.'

Joe thought about George Fern.

'He might have been involved in something else,' she said. 'Something back home. I think he had other interests.' She sighed.

After a moment, Joe said, 'I'm just curious why you're so forthcoming.'

'I need help.'

'In what way?'

'I need to get out of here.'

'Why did Dad come here the week before Christmas?'

'To see that I was all right. He said it wouldn't be for much longer.'

'What wouldn't?'

'Me being stuck here.'

'Did Dad ever mention Sheffield?'

She squinted at him. 'I don't think so. But he was just Jesse, you know . . .' She fanned the tears in her eyes. 'He told me he kept you and your mother in the dark. But when I heard about the crash, I knew you would be over here and I knew you would find me. I would have to tell you . . .'

'And if I hadn't come?'

She began to cry. 'But you did . . .' She stood up, walked to the water, and dived in. He watched her swim out, sticking close to the beige rocks and the curved arm of the breakwater.

He watched her swim away.

SILENT AS a cat, Rabbit paced the house, her new daily wanderings. She was surprised a track hadn't been worn into the carpet between the bed and window.

She hadn't been outside in days. She wouldn't dress. She spent hours in the bath and then slipped back into her nightie and dressing gown. She avoided looking in the mirror.

Kate kept texting. *What's wrong? What have I done? Answer your bloody phone.*

She watched the world of the estate pass through the screen of her bedroom window, always a watchful eye on the street. She pulled a chair over to the window and sat there, waiting for him, staring at the clouds passing overhead, watching birds roosting, squabbling in the garden. But there was no one lurking around, no suspicious cars, no one in the bushes with a pair of high-powered binoculars.

She slept whenever she wanted to sleep, but for no more than a couple of hours at a time. She was scared of having that dream again, of being pursued through the snow.

Her days felt twisted. Like time had begun to fray.

Cass followed her around the house, fretting, fussing.

'I'm going to call the doctor.'

'No more doctors,' Rabbit said.

'I can't keep ringing the factory for you. They said you need a sick note after three days. Do you want to get the sack?'

The temperature had dropped again, as if the season were reflecting her mood, beginning to deepen. But the weather was just another non-event that happened outside her bedroom window, a mere backdrop for the things to come.

She watched a couple of teenagers cycling across the road from her window. The girl, her hair a long brown wave behind her, clung limpet-tight to the boy pedalling, his body tilted forward as if to make the bike go faster. It reminded her of herself and Frankie when they were young. She wished she could return to that time. A period when twilight was the only clock you needed to worry about. Getting home before the street lights came on.

All night long, the wind blew as if the planet had become unhinged. Wind against the house, whistling along the window ledge, howling around the gables. Winds coming down off Cuckoostone Moor like wild horses, trampling gardens, pushing against trees and bending them like twigs.

Around 9 a.m. the next morning, she went downstairs to find Cass making cheese on toast in the kitchen. She was in a strop.

'The factory's been on the phone again.'

'OK. Call the doctor. Get me a sick note.'

'Really?'

'Yeah, really. Anything to stop your griping.'

*

181

The doctor, formal in his brown suit and plain blue tie, asked her to loosen her clothes and lie on the bed. He touched her stomach with his cold, liver-spotted hands, as if he were kneading dough.

'Is there anything you'd like to talk to me about?' he asked.

In the dim light of the room, the doctor's open face appeared serene in the space above her. She had looked at this face when she was a young girl, this doctor who had been with her through her childhood ills – warts, measles, chickenpox, tonsillitis, head lice – and felt the same sense of peace.

'I keep thinking about him,' she said. 'The traces of him. When I was pregnant, we made lots of things. Toys, clothes.'

The doctor nodded.

'I keep trying,' she said, 'but it's such a struggle.'

'Maybe you went back to work too soon? I'll sign you off for a fortnight. And if you're still not feeling up to it after that, come and see me and we can have a chat. OK?'

He squeezed her hand and gave her a leaflet for a support group in Chesterfield.

When Sudden Death Occurs

RABBIT WATCHED the street, waiting for Frankie. It was empty. No cars, no movement. She walked back to bed. A little while later, the doorbell rang. Footsteps. Frankie knocked and shouldered his way in, clutching a carrier bag full of gifts.

'Here you go.' He slung the bag on the bed. 'Your five a day.'

Rabbit smiled. In it was a bottle of red wine, a large bar of chocolate, the latest Hello! magazine, some bath salts and a spliff.

'Thanks.'

She tried to deflect the inevitable conversation with questions. What's the gossip at the factory? Have you seen Kate at all? As if hiding in her bedroom was completely normal. The way she spoke, looking beyond him.

He told her he was having to cadge a ride to the factory from Jergen, the old Swedish bloke who worked in the deep freeze, who had a silvery quiff and carbolic complexion.

It was nice to think about something else for a while.

He said, 'I told Fat Heather I'd help out on your line while you were away.'

'You didn't have to do that.'

He snorted. 'Wish I hadn't. They think I'm being keen. Showing initiative. The fuckers have only gone and offered me a promotion.'

'Oh no. What?'

'There's a SPAM vacancy coming up.'

Selector Panel and Mix specialist. If ever there was a duller job; connecting pipe work; doing temperature checks on each vat every three hours; sending samples to the lab. Yawn. There'd be no more getting stoned during a break or driving to the pub for a swift pint.

He asked, 'Look, all of this, is it owt to do with Kate? Because she's a stuck-up little cunt, if you ask me.'

'No . . . No, it's not.'

Frankie looked at her. 'You know that day we drove to your old house.'

'Yeah?'

'You said you had something to tell me.'

Although the words formed in her head, they wouldn't come out of her mouth. The thought of getting him involved. It was too late; she'd left it too long. It was foolish, selfish. She dismissed it sharply and her mood deflated. But she hated lying to him.

'I'm sorry. I can't do this now. Can we drop it?'

Later, she smoked the spliff while peeking from behind the curtains. She flicked the burning roach out of her bedroom window, watching it spark as it hit the side of the house. She could smell the funk of her bedroom mixing with the fresh air, air that smelled metallic, watery. It filled her with a sense of longing. To be away from this valley.

There was no need for an inquest, they'd said. She had to pay to see a report written in gobbledegook, which the paediatrician had to go through with her and explain. They asked if she wanted to visit his body before they took him to the mortuary. No. She didn't want to see his face again. He would feel different, she just knew he would.

Cass said she would go and see him one last time. Rabbit asked her to cut a lock of his hair and to take some hand- and footprints. Keepsakes. Rabbit had the prints framed, but they've lain in a drawer ever since. They scattered his ashes on Jawbone Lake.

She slept for a while and then took up her place at the window, pleased to see it was still night-time.

She saw movement on the pavement outside. A cat's silhouette turning circles in the flat pool of light beneath the street lamp. It was her cat, Socks. But when she opened the window to call out his name, he'd gone.

She closed the window, drew the curtains, and opened the bottle of wine. Shortly after, she heard the floorboards going, the squeak of the stairs, and a sleepy Cass appeared, sleep-dishevelled hair sticking up at one side.

'Sorry, did I wake you?'

Cass shook her head. 'Bad dream.'

'What about?'

She eyed the bottle; smiled. 'You going to pour me a glass, or what?'

As Joe wandered alone along the pontoons, among the costly yachts, all he could register was a growing sense of unease in the fact that the CJ who Beatriz was describing, and the world he inhabited, was a million miles from the man he thought he knew. How are you meant to react when you find out that your father is involved in the world of organised crime? How are you meant to reconcile this new version of your father with the old? Would it all come out one day? Would everyone know?

Joe felt the shame on a cellular level. Like his DNA had been stained.

She was in the shower when he got back to the yacht. He opened his MacBook and went to Google Earth. He scanned the Kent coastline near Hastings.

That must be it. Dungeness.

He phoned Bill.

'So what's she like then, this Beatriz? As pretty as in her photograph?'

Joe sighed. 'There's much more to it than Beatriz. This company of Dad's. You knew it was bent, didn't you?'

'Eh?'

'She reckons Dad was laundering money,' Joe said.

Bill was silent for a while, contemplating the information.

'What?' Joe asked. 'You knew?'

'Knew? No. I certainly did not.'

'You never spoke to Dad about it?'

'I kept my nose out.'

'You don't seem that surprised.'

Bill sighed. 'I had my suspicions. But never this. Laundering? No way. Has this got something to do with the crash?'

'I don't know. Dad had some dirt on these people he was involved with, these Stone brothers. One of them claims he owes him money. But I don't think they'd want anything bad to happen to him.'

'You mean CJ was blackmailing them?'

'Uh-huh. Are you sure you've never heard of them?'

'That's what I'm telling you, youth. No.'

'Beatriz seems to think he was involved in something else. Do you think the police know any of this?'

'I'm sure we'd have heard about it, if they did.'

'You think so?'

Bill was silent.

'Look, I'm coming home,' Joe said.

'When?'

'Soon as I can get a flight.'

'OK. But listen.'

'What?'

'Don't be telling your mother owt. Not until we know for certain.' He hung up.

Joe should have been relieved in some way, to know

about the fallout with the Stone brothers, the whole affair with the money laundering, but he wasn't. Beatriz's smiles, her feline movements, her knowledge of everything – it all seemed a little bit too self-contained, too easily explained.

But things were starting to fall into place. Whenever CJ walked into a room, people would sense his presence, they would turn to look at him, maybe not all at once, but gradually their eyes would be drawn to him. It was his bulk, the way he carried himself. When Joe was growing up, he noticed men would always defer to CJ, seek his opinions, repeat his name unnecessarily. *How you doing, CJ? I agree, CJ.* Joe was always 'CJ's lad'. *Next time you talk to CJ, tell him I was asking after him.* Joe had thought this was completely normal, if a little embarrassing. Because you have to be reverent. You have to show respect. Now he knew why.

He wondered how the hell he was going to tell her.

He found Beatriz sitting on the coachroof of the yacht. Her hair was tied back and she had her legs drawn up, arms folded, elbows on knees. She was wearing a white vest top and Capri pants and sandals, the picture of elegance.

'I thought we could go to the clubhouse this afternoon,' she said.

'I'm leaving,' he said.

'Look, why don't you relax a little? I miss him too. But do you think he'd just want us to hide ourselves away and stop living?' She reached over and touched his forearm. 'We're both in the same boat.'

'Is that mean to be funny?'

'Suit yourself.' She climbed down into the cockpit and

stood facing him. 'Jesse always spoke so highly of you,' she said, smiling.

'Take the yacht,' Joe said.

'What?'

'Take the boat. Get out of here. Sail up the coast.'

'I've got no money.'

'But you're partying at the clubhouse every day.'

'I've got a bit, yes. But it's going to run out soon. Jesse was going to help me.'

'Then sell it. The yacht. I want nothing to do with it.'

Joe stared into those dark eyes, trying to gauge her sincerity.

'Can you tell me something?' he asked.

She sighed, hands on hips. 'What?'

'Describe Lawrence to me. What does he look like?'

'Beard. Bald head. Muscles.'

They stared at each other in silence.

'Is that it?' she asked.

He nodded.

She clambered over the guardrail and clomped down the pontoon. He watched her until he couldn't see her any more and then headed down into her cabin. Still the same mess. Clothes, perfume, make-up. A folder full of papers, in Spanish. Jewellery in a small wooden box. He peered under her bed and spotted a leather holdall, free of the dust it was surrounded by. Inside, he found money, and beneath it, a pistol.

It was cold, heavy, hideous.

He put it back in the holdall, zipped it up, and placed it back under the bed.

He collected his things and headed along the pontoons

to the security cabin. He asked the guard to book him a taxi to the airport. Five minutes later, the taxi arrived. Partway through the journey, he got his iPhone from his bag and pressed Rose's number.

'Joe. What do you want?'

'Can you speak?'

After a minute, she said, 'Uh-huh.'

'Why didn't you just tell me?'

'What?'

'About Dad. What he was up to out here. His dealings with Robert and Lawrence. Hastings. Gypsies. Drugs. Money laundering. Do I need to go on?'

'It wasn't my place . . .'

'Lawrence thinks Dad's alive. Do you?'

'I can't imagine what you've been going through.'

He snorted a laugh. 'The hell you can't. This is your life, isn't it? The chaos of crime.'

'I'm sorry. We all loved your dad.'

'And what about Robert?'

'I can't talk about that.'

'So where is Lawrence?'

'He was so upset when CJ burned his bridges.'

'What about the money he wants me to pay back?'

'Forget that.'

'That's easy for you to say. And Beatriz?' he asked. 'She said nothing went on between them, but I'm not sure I believe her.'

'CJ's known her since she was a little girl. She took a real shine to him. It was CJ that paid for her English lessons. He wanted her to do well in the world. Get out of the village. Get away from here.'

'Why?'

'Oh, I don't know. Because he was a good guy?'

'Whatever.'

'Listen,' she said. 'CJ told me he never wanted this life. The deeper he got involved, the harder it got to leave.'

'You mean the easier it got to lie to us.'

'He was trying to protect you.'

'I don't know where these files are, OK. This paper trail leading to Lawrence. Maybe Dad never even had them in the first place, have you considered that? Maybe he was bluffing.'

'There's no need to be melodramatic,' she said.

'Did Lawrence have anything to do with the crash?'

Silence. A quiet 'No'.

'So there's no point me going to the police?'

'Feel free. But you're asking the wrong questions. You should be asking yourself why CJ closed the operation down. None of us know.'

After a moment, Joe asked, 'Did Dad smoke weed?'

She laughed gently. 'Don't sound so surprised. It's a little indulgence, that's all. I grow it at the house. I'd give him an ounce now and then. He was funny when he was high. A real blast.'

'So people keep telling me. You and my dad,' he said. 'You never . . . you know?'

He imagined her salacious, cougarish grin.

'You'll never know.'

'So is that it, then?' he asked. 'Is everything over?'

She took a while to answer. 'I guess.'

'Well, make sure you tell Lawrence.' He hung up.

HER NAME was Rebecca Miller. Thirty-two years old, though she looked younger. An operative at the ice-cream factory. She lived with her auntie. There was no man around, just a young chav off the estate who visited occasionally, probably her boyfriend. She hadn't been to work the past couple of days. Spent far too much time peeking through her curtains.

Grogan kept his distance.

She hadn't told anyone, that much was for sure. The way she kept looking out of the window. She was afraid. No one to protect her. No one to run to.

But he had to be sure.

And then he'd end it.

Week Six

As Joe walked to the allotment, he thought about what he was going to say. There were still so many gaps. He still couldn't explain the crash, the anonymous call, the journey from Sheffield that night. Maybe he had to start at the beginning, from the moment CJ left the valley and moved to Hastings; the fight in Lawrence's club.

It was the inevitable fate of the eavesdropper, discovering things you ought not to know. But it was only a matter of time before the arc of CJ's secret life intersected the arc of theirs.

He never suspected CJ's business fell on the wrong side of the law, and he wasn't even sure how to feel about it now that he knew. Cleaning drugs money, of all things. He should have been upset, disappointed, but he wasn't — he just felt numb.

This was Joe's inheritance. Silence upon silence, stones piled upon stones. Bill had bequeathed to CJ this secretiveness, which CJ, in turn, had bequeathed to Joe.

He needed someone to talk to because mulling all of this over, on his own, really wasn't helping. His thoughts led him to a certain point and he couldn't go any further.

He knew no one could put it into perspective – it had gone beyond that – but he just needed someone to bounce ideas off. Maybe he could phone Sarah – not that she ever answered any more. She'd met CJ many times and they'd got on so well. CJ said Joe should have married her when he had the chance.

This was just another moment when he realised he didn't know anyone that well any more. Something had happened a few years ago, when things had turned sour between him and Sarah, when he stopped fully connecting with the world.

But he wasn't going to be like that any more, he told himself.

Through the window in the little dark shed at the allotment, Joe could see Bill sitting in his worn armchair, a brown huddle of tweed.

He pushed open the door. Bill looked up. 'Well well well.'

Joe looked at the furze of Bill's beard, the long hairs of his eyebrows. His eyes were sinking into their sockets, but they were quick and seemed to be checking Joe's face for something.

Bill climbed out of his chair and started touching his tools, counting them under his breath.

'So what do we do now?' he asked Bill.

Bill shook his head. 'I don't know, youth. I've thought of nowt else.'

'Should we go to the police?'

'No,' Bill snapped. 'Not yet, anyway.'

'Do you have any phone numbers or addresses,' Joe said, 'for any of Dad's old friends down in Hastings?'

'Your mother might. She said someone from Hastings phoned a few days ago, to offer his condolences.' Joe wondered if it was Lawrence. 'She might have a number. Why?'

'I'm just thinking of going down there, seeing what I can find. Seeing if I can find anything else out, I mean.' Joe paused. 'Dad's friend, the one that died when he was young . . .'

'George Fern?'

'That's him.'

'None of this has got owt to do with George. He died when they were both sixteen.'

'How come I never heard his name before?'

Bill shrugged his bony shoulders. 'They were like brothers. Always together. George is the reason CJ left the valley.'

'He never talked to me about it.'

Bill folded his arms and began to recount the day of George's funeral. 'People were standing in the aisles, lining the streets, tipping hats and heads as the hearse rolled by. I never realised young George had touched so many.' He stared down at his shaking hands, as if surprised to find himself so old. 'The father dies before the son,' Bill said. 'That's the deal.'

His watery eyes stared at Joe.

'George's dad still lives over in Musdale,' Bill said. 'The farmhouse on the edge of the crags. You should pay him a visit.'

Joe nodded. 'So why did Dad go to Hastings, of all places?'

'We used to go down there for summer holidays.'

'I just thought he'd chosen some random place on the map.'

'No.' Bill blinked at Joe with his apple-green eyes. 'It's up for sale.'

'What is?'

'My house. They put the sign outside this morning.'

'It's for the best, Grandad. You know it is.'

Bill nodded for a while. 'Aye.'

'Where's Mum? She's not at home.'

'She'll be at her friend Janet's house. She's there all the time nowadays.'

Joe laid a hand on Bill's bony shoulder, squeezed once, and then opened the shed door and peered down the slope of the allotment towards the river. A tired-looking heron stood sentry on the bank opposite, eyeing the water. Most of the snow had melted over the past two weeks and the river was in spate.

He wondered how present CJ ever really was. Which life did he inhabit or prefer? The family in the Peaks, or his secret life in Andalusia? Were they just converse, but complementary halves of the same life, the same self? As far as Joe knew, he was just collecting further knowledge of CJ, accumulating and assimilating a fuller picture of him. Yet that's all it was: fuller, but still incomplete.

The heron took flight, its spindly body reflected in the water. Something prehistoric about it. Something ultimately sad.

Early the next morning, Joe turned on his bedside lamp and scanned the room, searching for clues. Often lately, he woke in the night and didn't know where he was.

He climbed out of bed, walked over to the window, and could just make out the crackle of stars above the valley.

He checked Eileen's room; she still wasn't back. He went downstairs, made himself a cup of coffee, then headed back up to bed. He got the parcel from the bedside cabinet and watched the second DVD again.

The journey up High Tor.

Later, sitting in the living room, he stared through the bay window at the willow tree in the front garden. Around him, Bill's stacks stood high. The paper, mainly newspapers and magazines, lent the house a heavy, inky smell. It had only taken Bill two weeks to take over the room completely.

He spotted Eileen walking up the garden path, clutching a carrier bag to her chest.

She wafted into the room smelling of perfume and hairspray, and gave him a hug.

'I'm so glad you're back, son. I've missed you. You've caught the sun.'

They went through to the kitchen and she put the kettle on. She seemed so much happier than the last time he'd seen her. If only she knew. She passed him a mug of hot, sweet coffee, sat on the stool at the breakfast bar, and stared down into her cup.

'So you've nothing to tell me,' she said.

Joe paused. 'No. I'm afraid not. Sorry.'

'So it was a wasted trip, then?'

'I wouldn't say that.'

'And this Beatriz?'

'I told you. They were just friends.'

'Don't lie to me. I can handle it, Joe.'

'There's a difference between being a flirt and a cheat, Mum.'

'He was certainly a flirt.'

'There was nothing going on between them,' he said, 'I'm sure of that. CJ had known her since she was a little girl, that's all. She's only in her early twenties. You were the love of his life.'

Eileen nodded. 'What should we do with the casita?'

'I've no idea. Leave it for now, I guess.'

They were silent for twenty, thirty seconds. Joe nodded towards the stack of paper in the corridor outside.

'I know,' Eileen said. 'I've spoken to him about it. The funny thing is, he doesn't see magazines or flyers or free newspapers. It's like he sees all the bad things he's ever done, put right. Like they keep the house safe from harm. He likes to count them, touch them, sniff them.'

Joe stared at the stacks.

Eileen said, 'You know what everyone thinks, don't you?'

'About what?'

'They think CJ's faked the whole thing.'

'Who cares? Don't listen to them.'

'Well, I just don't know what to make of it all.' Eileen looked surprised by what she'd just said.

'Mum, come on.' Joe paused. 'He wouldn't do that to us.'

She sighed. 'I know. But still. It's what people are saying.'

Joe drummed his fingers on the worktop.

'I was talking to Grandad earlier, and we got talking about why Dad left the valley when he was sixteen. George Fern.'

'What about him?'

'I just wondered why CJ never told me about him.'

'With all that's happened, you're asking me about George Fern?' She squinted at him.

'I just want to know, that's all.'

'They were like brothers. Always together.' She rubbed her neck nervously, eyes turning over memories that Joe wanted to share. 'George went out climbing without your dad one day and never came back. Some walkers found him the next day. He'd fallen. Broken his neck.' Eileen paused. 'And broke your dad's heart. CJ just couldn't stand being here any more. Everywhere he looked, he saw George. That's why he left Ravenstor and bobbied off down south. He blamed himself, you see. They'd been arguing the week before.'

'What about?'

Eileen folded her hands in her lap. 'It was at the Social Club. I was there with my pals. CJ and George turned up on George's motorbike with their leather jackets and long hair. All the girls watching them. The band were awful and kept messing up the songs, but no one seemed to mind. We were all drunk and dancing away.

'CJ had this young slip of a thing following him around all evening. She was probably only fourteen, wearing a miniskirt and low-cut top. We were all dancing together – but she was all over him. Then CJ disappeared off to the bar, and George stepped in, smoking a cigarette, flirting. She took the cigarette off him and blew smoke into his face, laughing. CJ spotted them. He ran over and clocked George, good and proper.'

'What's that got to do with George's death?'

'They'd made plans to go out the following Saturday, to

a party up at Nine Sisters, the stone circle. They were meant
to be camping over. I think George assumed CJ was going
and so he stayed away. Your dad thought the same, and so
he stayed in. Playing dominoes with Grandad, he said.'

A knock at the front door made them both jump.

Eileen tutted. 'See who it is, will you?'

Joe opened the door to find Father Jones, the minister,
standing there.

'I don't mean to intrude,' he said.

Joe nodded. 'Father Jones,' he said, loud enough for
Eileen to hear in the kitchen. 'Come in.'

The minister stepped into the house, wiping his brogues
on the mat. Joe noticed he had some kind of product in
his Bible-black hair that made it clump together in fat
strands.

They walked into the kitchen. Eileen looked up from
the kettle. 'Oh, minister,' she said. 'It's good of you to drop
by. I'm sorry for the way I behaved that day. There's no
excuse.'

'It's fine. Don't worry.'

'Can I get you a drink? Tea, coffee . . . something
stronger?'

'I can only stay a minute, I'm afraid.' The minister paused,
as if taking in the dimensions of the room. The kitchen
was warm and smelled of toast, Eric Clapton's 'Layla' playing
quietly on the radio station. 'I know things must be difficult,'
he said, eyeing them both in turn. 'The fact that they haven't
found CJ yet. But I was wondering if you've thought about
holding a memorial service. For CJ's life. For you and the
family, and the people in the valley. He was well liked.'

To hold us up for closer inspection, Joe thought.

Eileen sighed, looking at Joe. 'I don't know,' she said. 'We'll have to talk to Bill.'

'Of course.'

'CJ wasn't religious,' Joe said. 'None of us are.'

'Sure. But it doesn't have to be religious.'

Meaning there would be no talk of the pitfalls of losing one's faith, or straying from the path of righteousness. If only they knew.

The minister said, 'We can plan it so that it reflects who CJ was.'

Eileen stared at the man stonily. 'Was?'

'I'm sorry. I mean . . .'

Still waiting for his body to appear, trapped in this state of siege, of present tense.

'We just miss him,' Eileen said. 'That's all.'

The minister nodded, and then said, 'Speak to Bill and let me know. And please, if you need anything, anything at all, you know where I am.'

Joe walked over to the kitchen window and stared into the back garden, towards the summer house. Behind him, Eileen said, 'Thank you,' and showed the minister to the door.

Mr Fern lived in an old farmhouse on the edge of the woodland that tumbled down into Musdale. At the entrance to his front garden there was a hand scythe lodged in a gatepost as if left from a bygone age. There was an old, beat-up Datsun in the drive, grass and weeds growing out of the smashed windscreen. Beside it, a punchbag hung from a tree. Scrawny chickens were pecking and clucking around a dirt-splattered quad bike and there were car doors leaning against a ramshackle aviary, a lean-to at the side of the house covered in green tarpaulin. Crags curved around the back of the house, as if embracing it.

Joe knocked on the front door. A dog barked once and then yelped.

The man who answered had a shock of white hair, an electric-blue tracksuit and tinted aviator glasses. 'What do you want?' he asked.

'I'm Joe Arms. CJ's son.'

Mr Fern removed his glasses. His gaze sucked all thought from Joe's head.

'So you are,' he said. 'Sorry. Come on in, duck. Take a load off.'

The inside of the house was tidy, though there was a fug of wet dog and tobacco in the air. The decor was a mishmash of ugly, large wooden furniture and psychedelic carpets.

'Park your arse, son. Can I get you a drink? All I've got's water and whiskey.'

'I'm fine, thanks.'

He poured himself a finger and sat opposite Joe, sipping and sighing. Joe noticed dark grease stains on the crocheted, brightly coloured antimacassar hanging on the back of his chair, and then the whites of Mr Fern's ankles. He wasn't wearing any socks.

'Sad fucking affair with CJ, if you don't mind me saying so.' The dog whimpered in the other room. 'How's your mother coping?'

'As well as can be expected.'

He snorted, leaned back in his chair, and peered down at the amber liquid in his glass. 'It's funny,' he said, 'the way they carried on, CJ and George. Their matching hair, clothes, and that, always on a motorbike together, you could easily mistake them for brothers. Like blood.'

Joe nodded.

'You know about George, do you? You want to see his room?'

Mr Fern stood with a groan and headed for the stairs.

There were bits of old climbing equipment lying around the bedroom, a large Spider-Man poster above the bed, and what looked like parts of a motorbike engine dotted along a sideboard. Everything looked shiny and new, dusted and polished regularly. Covering one wall were postcards and photographs of local landmarks, mainly crags and escarpments towering out of forest.

'He was an avid photographer,' Mr Fern said. 'I reckon once he'd got climbing out of his system, he could have made a career out of photography. Maybe combined the two. CJ was keen on it too, making his little films and that. You still got any of those?'

'Yeah.'

'That's Black Rocks. Hanging Holes. And that's Stanedge, where it all started. Climbing, I mean. Back in Victorian times. Did you know that?'

Joe shook his head.

Mr Fern turned back to the photographs: Rowtor Rocks. Hermits Cave. King Stone. Eagle Tor. Castle Ring. Nine Ladies. Then he pointed at a small, square, colour photograph. 'This was taken up at Druid's Inn. They used to go up there a lot on George's scrambler. Cut across the fields, no helmets on. Get pissed as ferrets. It was the only place that'd serve them underage.' Mr Fern tutted and Joe could smell the whiskey on his breath. 'You telling me you grew up around here and you've never been up to Birchover or Stanton Moor?'

'Maybe. With my dad.'

'You see George's shiner? That was taken the week before he died.'

Joe stared at George's black eye, trying to imagine himself into the photograph.

Mr Fern chuckled. 'CJ gave George the shiner. They'd been scrapping over some bit of skirt. But George, he were always covered in cuts and bruises from the rocks. A climber, you see. I guess CJ told you?'

Joe shrugged. Chickens began squabbling outside the window.

'Free soloing,' Mr Fern said. 'No ropes or harnesses. No safety equipment. You need serious balls. We used to fret, but what can you do? The back garden is basically a climbing wall. We could hardly keep him locked indoors all day. Were a free spirit, he was. His mother, she used to berate him all the time. But he said he loved the sense of loneliness up there. It were Robin Hood's Leap what started it all. We used to take him up there when he was a kid. He loved it. Like a little mountain goat he were, a real crag hopper. You'd swear he had suckers for hands. But he died doing what he loved and I've come to take some comfort in that over the years. There was no one in the valley who weren't shocked by his fall.'

Mr Fern peeled the photograph from the wall and handed it to Joe.

'You can have it, duck. CJ would like that. Never stop remembering George. CJ always used to come visit. He was a grand fucking fella. He was proud of you and all. You know that, don't you?'

Joe smiled. 'Yes.'

'Paid for a plaque, your dad did, along the Giddy Edge. Put it up a few years back. To commemorate. I liked that. Like George is still up there, dangling by his fingertips. Grinning into the sky.'

Joe CLIMBED the meadow on the eastern flank of High Tor's summit, the path CJ recorded on the Super 8, the world of the journey framed, channelled back through time. The wind got stronger the higher he got. As he neared the edge, a sign on a post in the ground warned: SHEER DROP KEEP WELL BACK FROM THE EDGE.

He stepped as close as he dared, feeling sick as he peered down the 120-metre drop to the River Derwent below. He stepped back and watched three white pods of the alpine chairlift climbing the Heights of Abraham, catching his breath. Beyond that, the S-shaped valley snaked towards the hill at Wirksworth where the radio mast stood beside Black Rocks.

He looked everywhere for a plaque but all he could find were the occasional signs nailed to posts, signs for grottos, crevices and crags, or warnings: CAUTION DEEP CHASM, accompanied by a human figure being swallowed by the earth.

He headed down the opposite side of the tor. Above him, the naked branches of the ash-elms appeared super-imposed against the sky. Partway down, he spotted an entrance overgrown with bushes, and the smallest of way signs, barely noticeable, beside a narrow mud track.

GIDDY EDGE ONE-WAY SYSTEM
NO ENTRY

The path became narrower, leading through a tunnel of overhanging branches and crag. He had to duck and pat-a-cake along the jagged rock face to his right. The path curved then widened out enough for a bench, constructed from three strips of wood. Joe sat down, breathing heavily, back claggy with sweat, and stared out towards the shadowy woodland on the opposite side of the valley.

The plaque, fixed to a knee-high piece of wood beside the bench, read:

George Adam Fern
Died whilst climbing on 17 June 1969
He touched the lives of many
Remembered with love and affection

Joe removed the photograph from his shirt pocket and laid it against the plaque.

He imagined CJ sitting there, staring into the space between the two hillsides, the space that hope disappeared into. The place where it all began, where CJ's life took a detour, a wrong turn.

If George and CJ hadn't been fighting over some girl. If CJ had apologised to him that week and gone to the party with him the following Saturday. If they had set up a business together . . .

He needed to keep following the trail of CJ's flight from the valley, from the remorse it held. He needed to go to Hastings and find out if Lawrence still lived there. Find out more about the early days, the Stone brothers and CJ working together. Was there anything else he didn't know? Was anyone else involved? Or was he just picking at scabs?

He imagined CJ sitting there, rerunning the fight at the Social Club, throwing the first punch, catching George just above the left ear. A girl screaming. Eileen turning to look as her future husband took another swing at George and the band kept playing.

Swallow the grief.

Keep him safe.

SHE GLANCED at the numbers on her digital clock, 04:23, and saw five lots of consecutive numbers adding up to 423.

211 + 212
140 + 141 + 142
68, 69, 70, 71, 72, 73
43 to 51 and 15 to 32

Mental arithmetic, mental gymnastics. The numbers salved her. They made her feel like there was order in the world. When she was a little girl, she would pick a number and use it all day. Three slices of bread and jam for breakfast. Three taps of her shoe on each paving stone along the school path. Three *Amens* at the end of morning assembly.

Should she just get up? she wondered. Get dressed and head to the factory. Immerse herself in the monotony of it, the mind-freeze of working the line. Daydreaming. Clock-watching. Hoping he wasn't following her.

She leaned over, lifted a pen from her bedside table, and held the nib an inch from the skin on the back of her hand. I'll measure my day by this, she thought. It will be my happiness barometer. Nought being miserable, ten ecstatic.

The alarming quiet of the house was a whoosh in her ears. There was no blare resounding from the telly and she hadn't heard Cass coming up the stairs yet. She pictured Cass sat on the settee fretting about her, and a stab of self-reproach shuddered through her. Because this was how Rabbit saw herself: a burden.

She wrote the number on the back of her hand in blue biro.

3

Three, with its beginning, middle and an end.

The doorbell again. Footsteps on the landing. Not Cass. Her bedroom door opened a crack. Kate's head appeared around it. 'Can I come in?' There she was, standing in Rabbit's doorway with a look of concern that could so easily be mistaken for love.

She wafted into the room smelling of fresh air and Nina Ricci. Kate perched on the edge of the bed.

'Here. I got you a little present,' she said.

'You shouldn't have.'

'Just open it.'

Rabbit removed the perfectly wrapped brown paper. A book. *The Man Who Loved Only Numbers*.

'He was a Hungarian maths genius. I think it might be right up your street.'

'Thanks. I haven't read a book in ages.'

Kate stared at Rabbit's hand. 'What's the number mean?'

Rabbit shrugged. 'Nowt. Can I have a hug?'

They held each other briefly and then Kate stood up and removed her coat. 'Everyone's been asking after you at work.'

'That's nice.'

'So what's wrong? Why have you been avoiding me? Is this some kind of payback?'

Rabbit sucked in her lips and then finger-combed her hair. 'No. I'm thinking of moving onto the late shift, permanently.'

Kate's smile melted. 'Why? That would be horrible.'

'So I could see more of you.'

She felt Kate bristle.

'Don't be daft.'

'I like you,' Rabbit said. 'You know that.'

'I'm going to university in September. What's the point in getting into anything serious?'

Rabbit had already bought Kate a card in Paperchase. A good-luck card. She would have plenty of time to work out what she was going to write inside it.

That was it. There was to be no unspoken protocol, no romance this summer. No walks on the moors, no lying in fields.

Rabbit said, 'I hate the way people try each other on like clothes, to see how they fit, how comfortable they are, and then move on and try something new. That's how you make me feel: like a blouse you've worn a few times and grown tired of.'

Kate tutted. 'What's up with you? It's like you want us to be a couple or something. And do what, move in together? Have a baby?'

'Yeah. Let's have a fucking baby.'

Kate held her breath. 'God. I'm sorry. I didn't mean . . .'

Rabbit cleared her throat. 'Since he died, I've not wanted to be with anyone. You're the only . . .' She paused.

Kate shrugged, awkwardly.

You're better on your own, Rabbit told herself. She was used to that. It made sense. Like she needed a girlfriend in this backwater.

Rabbit stared at the wall where the cot used to stand and said, 'I didn't hear him struggling or choking. I just picked him up in the morning, to cuddle him, like I always did. He was grey, his lips blue. He was totally lifeless. Cass said she heard me screaming but all I know is that I was running down the stairs and she had him on the kitchen table and was talking to someone on the phone. She was giving him mouth-to-mouth for what seemed like forever and all I could do was stand there and watch. Like it was happening to someone else. The paramedics turned up and Cass was holding me back while they checked him over. I didn't want them to touch him. Then they wrapped him up in a blanket and took him away.'

Kate reached towards her, touching the back of her hand.

'The next hour was a blur. I kept asking to see him but they said they needed to ask me some questions first. No one actually said to me, Your son, he's dead. Cass, she wanted to talk about him all the time. I didn't. I just turned in on myself. That's why I went straight back to work. To block things out. Become a robot. You know what the factory is like, you don't have to talk to anyone if you don't want to. I was scared I'd burst into tears and make a fool of myself. I was so fed up with people asking me how I was all the time. After we scattered the ashes, I had to spend each night in the room where he'd died. This room.

'I still talk to him. I write him letters. It's the things we'll never get to do together that really hurts.'

214

In a tear-thickened voice, Kate said, 'I'm so sorry.'

'And now there's all of this going on. I feel like I'm going mad. I need to tell someone.'

'About what?'

'Jawbone.'

'What about it?'

Holding her breath, Rabbit stared at the 3 on her hand. 'It's a special place to me. Always has been. I'm from the village beneath the lake. Coldwater. My ancestors and that.'

Rabbit lowered her head, hiding her thoughts behind her fringe.

'New Year's Eve. I just headed down there to see the year in on my own. Just to think. Away from everything.'

Kate looked stern, tense.

'I heard a noise,' Rabbit said. 'I wasn't sure what it was at the time. Fireworks or something. But then I knew what it was. Gunshots.'

'What are you telling me, Rabbit?'

Rabbit winked, clicked her fingers, and cleared her throat three times. 'I saw what happened at the lake that night. CJ crashing through the bridge and into the ice. I was the one who called the police.'

Ellipses . . . dot dot dot, dash dash dash, dot dot dot . . .

Kate edged away. 'There was someone shooting at him?'

'He was being chased by another car. I definitely heard shots being fired.'

'Is this some kind of joke?'

'I wish.'

Kate's eyes were guarded, suspicious. 'What happened to the other car?'

215

'He saw me. The man driving it. There was a full moon –' she lowered her lids for a second – 'when I close my eyes, I can still see everything. Lit in silver.'

Kate was silent.

'I started to edge away but I tripped in the snow and when I looked back he was watching me.' As she spoke, Rabbit kept thinking, I am subtracting myself from Kate, but I need to get this out of me. 'So I ran into the woods to get away. The snow was deep, I keep having nightmares about it. The man chasing me . . . I called the police from a phone box. But I shouldn't have run, should I? I should have tried to help.'

She felt her fear replaced by the grip of sorrow. What had she just done?

Kate's eyes looked a little wild. 'You've got to tell someone,' she said.

'No. I don't.'

'But you have to, Rabbit.' The adult dishing out wisdom to a child.

'I saw him. Last week. He killed CJ. What's to say he won't kill me?'

'And Eileen? Joe?' Kate asked. 'Don't you think they've got a right to know? Mum said Eileen's been thinking all sorts of things. Can you imagine what it's been like?'

'Look, I just needed to say the words out loud. Promise me you won't tell anyone, Kate. Promise.'

Kate fixed her gaze on Rabbit's. Rage danced in her eyes.

'My mother died when I was ten,' Rabbit said. 'And my son died when he was only four months old. I'm obviously a really bad person.'

This is where she now existed, Rabbit realised: in a state of pause, of hesitation. In the space between people, disconnected.

Rabbit opened her arms and they hugged again. Kate's hold was loose, unbalanced.

When she'd gone, Rabbit licked the back of her hand. Erased the 3.

THE STASIS of a late winter's afternoon in a seaside resort. The boredom climatic, palpable in the low cortex of grey cloud. The doldrums of a town waiting for the promise of sunshine and clear skies that would magically transform everything. Hastings resembled some woebegone postcard. Its image: a mile-long promenade of mainly boarded-up shopfronts.

Joe misspent much of his youth in the arcades of Buxton and Matlock Bath, playing Laser Quest and Mortal Kombat, but Hastings Pier had burned to the ground years ago and it looked like the council was hoping it would be blown into the sea by the next big storm. Posters on the entrance attested to the fact that some well-intentioned locals had formed a 'Save the Pier' group, but the posters were as faded and tattered as the town itself.

He walked up to the address Eileen had given him: Empire X. It was now a grotty pub. That said it all.

He continued on, past the double-decker promenade, found a bench to sit on and stared out to sea. A group of sneering girls walked by, cackling and drunk, a cadre of boys on BMXs hot on their tails.

The beach was nothing but a bank of uninviting pebbles, the sea black and dead. Hastings depressed the hell out of him. The endless cawing of seagulls; the abrasive, salty wind that made you feel like you were hanging onto the edge of the earth. He certainly couldn't imagine CJ ever enjoying it here. Another setting for CJ's other life. It didn't feel real.

He pictured CJ walking along the promenade in the early hours of the morning, a man with a lot on his mind, a man who couldn't sleep, his only company the sound of lapping waves in the darkness. Joe saw him as a scratchy, shadowy figure; CJ alive to him. He could smell his Hugo Boss aftershave, his sweat in the tangy brine of the sea, and a palpable sense of the Jekyll and Hyde CJ staring through his eyes, staring at this town where he'd started to build his house of cards, where everything felt like it had come to an end.

Joe thought about the saying that we live on in the memories of those who knew us. But what if those memories are false, or simply untrue? What if we only showed each friend a certain aspect of our personality? It meant there were many versions of us locked within other people's narratives.

He didn't want to be in this woeful town having such dismal thoughts. This search was ridiculous. The more he found out about his dad, the less he knew.

He entered the address Eileen had given him into his iPhone. Began walking.

They sat at the dining-room table drinking tea.

He got the feeling that he was in the company of

genuinely nice people — a rare feeling. Sattar and his wife, Asmina, were warm, welcoming and friendly-looking. There were many framed photographs in the room but the images were only of Asmina and Sattar. No family portraits. No children to be seen.

'So what do you think of Hastings?' Sattar asked. 'Have you been to the Old Town? The castle?'

Joe shook his head.

'CJ loved it here,' Asmina said. 'He especially loved the May Day run. Hundreds of motorbikes up and down the promenade. It's a great atmosphere. We were the first people that CJ met when he moved down. He used to come into our restaurant in St Leonard's all the time. Back then, we were the only Indian restaurant for miles. He had lots of girlfriends, as I'm sure you can imagine. He always loved the fancy-dress party after the May Day run. He had a big motorbike for a while.'

Sattar laughed, his eyes turning over the memories.

Joe tried to picture his father as a young man, racing up and down the promenade on his bike, long hair and leathers, a trail of broken hearts in his wake.

Joe opened his mouth, about to ask about the Stones, but kept quiet.

They finished their teas, and Sattar offered to show him the house. They walked upstairs to the attic room. Sattar closed the door behind them. 'The playroom,' he said, proudly. There was a Stealth Wireless gaming chair, an early-model Xbox connected to a huge plasma screen, an electric Fender guitar and amplifier, and a Potty Putter with some expensive-looking golf clubs.

'The Stone brothers,' Joe said.

Sattar eyed him curiously. Nodded. 'Them.'

'I wanted to ask you about them.'

Sattar touched Joe's arm. 'Thank you for not saying anything in front of Asmina.'

'So you know them?'

'Look, I know them, but I never got involved in that side of things.'

'What do you mean?'

'Shh. Keep your voice down. Asmina's got no idea.' Sattar moved his weight from foot to foot, peering towards the ceiling. 'CJ had been down here about a year, running the cinema, yeah? Everything was going well. Until he met those two. They were both involved in some very shady business. Lawrence used to own a nightclub; and CJ got talking to them one night – a bar fight, or something. And got suckered in. Rich overnight, more or less. But I can't tell you anything else. Whatever happened between them, well, CJ knew better than to let it slip to me.'

'Shady business? What do you mean?'

Sattar shrugged, weighing Joe's reaction.

'It's OK,' Joe said. 'I know. Drugs.'

'I hear they got mixed up in smuggling, but don't hold me to it. You can understand I wanted to keep my distance. They moved away not long after your dad, though I'm sure I've seen them back here. That's all I can tell you, my friend.'

'Do you know where Lawrence moved to?'

He shook his head. 'Abroad. I know some of the police here. Lawrence will be arrested as soon as he steps foot on English soil, I know that much.'

'Did CJ have any more friends down here, anyone else he kept in touch with?'

'No,' Sattar said. 'Sorry. I think me and Asmina are the last of his Hastings crowd.'

Sattar walked across the room, sat cross-legged on the carpet, and patted the space beside him. 'Come here.' As Joe sat down, he slid a small black leather case towards him.

'I'd like you to have this,' Sattar said.

Joe opened the case. Inside was a Super 8 camera.

'It was CJ's. He lent it to me years ago, and then told me to keep it. It was his very first Super 8. I don't use it any more, but everything still works. The lens is in tip-top condition.'

Joe lifted the camera out, a Kodak Ektasound 130.

'CJ got me into it,' Sattar said. 'His passion was infectious.'

He told Joe they used to go away for weekends together to shoot films, and Asmina used to joke they were having an affair. They'd make her sit through the movies. Oh look, she'd tease, some driftwood on the beach. Oh look, a dog. Sattar belly-laughed at the memories. 'There's something very special about Super 8,' he said. 'CJ used to say that it was like capturing daydreams.'

'He had a real thing for it,' Joe said.

'Please, take it,' Sattar said. 'You should have it. It would make CJ happy, I know it would.'

Joe nodded. 'That's sweet of you. Thanks.'

JOE TOOK the coast road towards Dungeness, driving through run-down barrack towns and past a military firing range – a long stretch of fenced-off dune with red flags flying, which he assumed meant they were testing arms. He passed a caravan park located beneath an electricity pylon, like something from an American B-movie, and inexplicably he felt like he wasn't sure what country he was in any more. The shale landscape of Dungeness was other-worldly. There were no trees anywhere, no shelter from the elements, but pretty soon he could see the enormous nuclear power station perched on the horizon like the Emerald City.

He dropped the car into second as he drove past Prospect Cottage, admiring the black shed of a house with its sunflower-yellow window frames and bizarre garden of beachcombed driftwood, flint and rubble.

He'd travelled that road before. He'd driven down with Sarah one weekend, shortly after he moved to London. She'd wanted to see Derek Jarman's hut. He pushed the memories from his mind.

He parked outside the Pilot Inn, in the shadow of the black lighthouse, and climbed out of the car as a rain-laden easterly began to blow. He put on his flat cap, turned up his collar, and followed the path in the direction of the power station, which was giving off an almost imperceptible electronic hum – an insect buzz you wouldn't want to focus on for too long. Beyond the footpath, against all odds, purple sea kale, red poppies and bits of gorse sprouted.

With his back to the power station, he stared out to sea towards France. He imagined the three of them standing where he was standing. CJ, Lawrence and Robert, young men listening in the darkness for the putter of an outboard engine, and he experienced a sudden disconnect with the man he thought he knew, anger replaced by disappointment.

Joe headed back to his car and checked his iPhone. Four missed calls from Bill.

'Where the bloody hell have you been?' Bill shouted.

'Why?'

'The anonymous caller. The one that saw the crash at the lake.'

'What about her?'

'Just get yourself back, youth. All hell's broke loose.'

THE KNOCKING wouldn't stop; a pulse of anger at the front door. She heard Cass's raised voice and then the sound of a woman shouting up the stairs.

'You come talk to me, girl!'

Rabbit slunk beneath her covers.

'I told you she's not here,' Cass screamed. 'Now get out.'

The front door slammed shut. Rabbit crawled over to the window and froze: Eileen Arms stormed down the garden path and then stopped in the street outside. Hands on hips, she stood looking back at the house, waiting.

Cass came into the room.

'Are you going to tell me what the fuck's going on?'

Rabbit turned and sat with her back to the wall. 'What did Eileen say?'

'She wasn't making any sense. She said she was going to call the police. She said you knew something.'

'I know nothing.'

'Then why is she knocking our bloody door down?'

'I've no idea. Someone's been telling lies.'

Cass folded her arms. 'She said you made the telephone call that night.'

225

Rabbit shook her head, picking at the weft of the carpet. Cass stood there for a long time, staring down at her.

She'd almost finished packing when there was a second round of knocking on the front door. She glanced through her window. A silver Mercedes.

It was him.

She crept over to her bedroom door and opened it a little, listening, the pulse increasing with each breath.

'I'm with the *Ravenstor Herald*.' A thick Yorkshire accent. 'I'm working on a story about the crash on New Year's Day. I was wondering if you've got a few minutes, just to answer a few questions.'

'Eh?'

'It won't take very long. Maybe I could come inside.'

'What's this got to do with owt?'

'The article is about what's happened to the community since. How it's affected everyone. Is your niece in?'

Rabbit's heart was racing. She felt sick.

'Listen, knobhead, I don't know you from bloody Adam. Jog on.'

'I can offer money for an interview.'

'Just piss off!'

Rabbit heard the door slam.

She dashed across her room, grabbing her case and handbag. She walked down the stairs, silently. She could hear Cass speaking on the telephone in the living room. Rabbit sighed, waiting, and then rushed out of the back door.

BEHIND THE windscreen, Grogan had a clear view of not only the street that Rabbit lived on, but also the two connecting streets. Soon the police would set up their observation point. They would be doing background checks, making applications to tap her phone, and he would have to retreat. He wormed a finger between his shirt buttons and touched the St Christopher on his chest.

He hadn't seen her leave. He removed his flat cap, rubbed his forehead, and then replaced it. He cradled the snub-nosed revolver in his lap. Felt his finger in the cold curve of the trigger. Imagined the lead caroming around her skull, tearing up the meat.

Then he saw her, crouching low, dashing to her Honda Civic.

He turned the ignition. Put the car into gear.

In the distance, the mountains presided, flanked by the dark, abstract shapes of pine forest. She turned the radio back on, expecting to hear her name: Derbyshire Police on the lookout for a Rebecca Miller, aged thirty-two. She took B-roads and back roads whenever she could, the grey ribbon of the road pushing through the hills and into the mountains, leading her away. She'd passed signs for Lancaster, Kirby Lonsdale, and now Kendal. Countryside streaming through the windscreen, flashing by.

When she reached the brow of a hill, she dropped the car down a gear, switched the indicator on, and pulled into the side of the road. She stepped out of the car and into the wind coming off the fells, humming in the parallel lines of electricity cables dropping down into the distance where everything appeared to meet.

On a B-road just north of Kendal, she checked her mobile. Twenty-three missed calls. She was exhausted. She needed to take a shower and have a lie-down. Tomorrow, maybe, she'd keep heading north. Scotland. She'd keep going. She'd have to.

JOE STOOD in the spare bedroom looking at Bill stretched out on the bed, one ankle over the other, hands folded across his chest. It felt strange seeing the old man lying there. He looked flustered, out of breath. Like he'd had a turn.

'I've been all over the shop looking for her.'

'Who?'

'This bloody Rabbit girl.' Bill sat up. 'She's the anonymous caller. She witnessed the accident. There's all sorts of bloody gossip flying around.'

'Like what?'

'Like shots were fired.'

'Someone was shooting?'

'The little bitch has disappeared. But we won't know owt until we find her. There's no point speculating. It might be complete nonsense.'

'But we know it's not nonsense. It makes complete sense.'

Bill eyed him steadily, eyes wet with tears.

'How come the police didn't know shots were fired?'

Bill shrugged. 'Fuckwits.'

'Where's Mum? I thought DI Slater was coming round?'

'He is –' Bill slid a glance at his clock – 'so be here at four. Eileen's at Janet's. She's the one that told her. Her daughter's friends with this Rabbit. Though Eileen thinks Kate knows more than she's letting on. You know Kate?'

'Kate who?'

'Weir. The police are interviewing her now.'

Joe shrugged. 'I don't think so. Is Mum OK?'

'What do you think?'

'Why has Rabbit run away?'

'I'm hoping we'll find out at four.'

'Do you know where she lives?'

'Nether Tor. With her Aunt Cass. You'll know her. Small woman, big gob. Tits made of brass. If you walk across the tops, approaching the estate from the moor road, down that overgrown twitchel.'

'I know where you mean.'

'There's the Social Club on the right-hand side and two houses directly at the bottom. Theirs is the left-hand one. There's an arch over the garden gate. A privet arch. I walked down there earlier on. No one answered, mind.'

He only knocked once and not too hard, because as he did he realised he probably shouldn't be there. He got the sense he was being observed. He took his wallet out, removed one of his business cards, and was about to push it through the letter box when he saw the curtains move in the corner of his eye.

The woman who answered looked stressed and puffy-faced. He recognised her immediately. One of the estate women no one messed with.

'I'm Joseph Arms. CJ's son.'

'I know who you are.'

'Can I come in?'

She narrowed her eyes, scanned the street in both directions, and then grabbed his arm and pulled him inside. The house was small and dark and smelled of alcohol and disinfectant. She stood before him with her arms folded and a mean look on her face. A martyred look.

'I've got bugger all to tell you,' she said. 'Rabbit's done nowt wrong, mind. You hear me? Nowt.'

'Is it true, she saw what happened at the lake?'

Cass nodded. 'Looks that way.'

'She needs to come back. She needs to talk to the police.'

Cass seemed to shrink. 'I know,' she said, 'I'll . . . I'll find her.' She began pushing him towards the door.

He pressed his card into her hand. 'Call me if you hear anything.'

Her face softened. 'I'm sorry about your dad, by the way.' She looked at the card and passed it back to him. 'Now get out.'

The door slammed behind him. He paused at the gate. He needed to see Rabbit. He needed to hear what she saw on New Year's Day, to hear it from her lips. Because within her, CJ's actions still had an earthly pulse.

Joe walked home to find Eileen, Bill and DI Slater sitting in the living room waiting for him.

'Mum,' Joe said.

Eileen looked distraught. She put her head in her hands, her shoulders hunched and rounded. 'I feel sick. I don't think I can bear this.'

The room fell silent. Eileen glared at the policeman.

231

'Kate must be mistaken,' she said. 'None of this can be right.'

'There was no evidence at the scene,' Slater said, 'or indeed on CJ's vehicle, to suggest that shots had been fired. However, until we speak to Rebecca . . . Rabbit—'

'But why would anyone want to hurt him?'

Joe asked, 'Is this anything to do with his trip to Sheffield on New Year's Eve?'

'We don't know.'

'Is this now a murder inquiry?'

'We're reopening the case.'

'Are the divers going out again?'

Slater glanced towards the window, as if trying to fix a picture of the lake in his mind, and said, 'No. We plan to drag a side-scan sonar through the lake. It's a robotic underwater vehicle, an imaging platform with high-res optical sensing, designed for deep waters. It'll scan the entire lake in a few days, popping up every few hours to transmit data back.'

Joe pictured a robotic eye, floating silently through the lake. Searching, recording, hunting. Then he pictured the bridge that night, adding a second vehicle to his familiar, imaginary tableau: he saw the pine wood hugging the lakeshore and, between the tree trunks, the headlights of the speeding vehicles flaring, guttering. He could see his father then; he could marry the man to Slater's words. Rabbit watching the scene from the lakeshore as the Land Rover smashed through the wall and plunged into the lake.

What kind of a death was that? Being chased, gunned down, crashing through a bridge. It certainly wasn't heroic.

CJ's life was a double exposure. He was a man who

never raised a hand to anyone, especially not to Joe – and yet there was something so violent about what he was engaged in.

Joe opened his mouth to speak. *The Stone gang*, he wanted to say. All eyes turned to look at him.

Bill shook his head, almost imperceptibly, just for Joe to see. Joe peered down at his hands.

Slater got to his feet, fastened the single button on his suit jacket, and said, 'We're doing everything we can to find Rabbit. You can call me on my number at any time, but I'll keep you posted with any information as it comes to us. I know it's a difficult time, but we'd appreciate it if you didn't speak to anyone about this.'

The three of them sat in silence. Bill walked over to the window, leaned against the windowsill, and stared out into the garden.

Eileen was gripping the chair arm so tightly her knuckles turned white. She broke the silence, a yellow flame of irritation in her eyes. 'It's true, isn't it? I can feel it in my bones. I was married to a liar. This town with its crises that come and go. I've always felt smug watching other people's lives become TV melodramas.'

'Mum.'

'And now it's my turn. And do you know what else, son? I look at you and I see him. I can't stand it. The Arms men, you're all the same. I never know what's going on inside any of your heads.'

Joe tried to put his arms around her but she shoved him away.

'Have you any idea how ashamed I am by all of this?

People will be whispering and pointing at me. Six weeks on, and CJ is about to ruin us. Just get out,' she said. 'The both of you. Get out and give me some peace.'

Joe touched Bill's arm as they left the house.

'Don't,' Bill said. 'I'm up to here with it all.'

'We need to talk.'

'Keep your voice down.'

'Let's go to the allotment.'

'No,' Bill said. 'There's nowt to discuss. Not until Rabbit's found.'

Joe watched Bill walk away and stood there for a few minutes, frozen to the spot, his mind so full of thought that nothing made sense. He wandered down through the twitchels towards the river. Black in the street lamps, the river ran so slow it looked like oil. Creatures scattered in the undergrowth, a scurrying through the nettles. He paused under a tree and watched the water slab against an upside-down shopping trolley. The creeping smell of rust, chemicals.

Did the Stones have anything to do with the crash on New Year's Day? Had Beatriz been lying to him about the paper trail, about the blackmail? Was it Lawrence in that other vehicle, chasing CJ, trying to shoot him dead?

The initial shock of what CJ was involved in had been replaced by this manic need to piece together the jigsaw of his life, the complicated unfurling of facts and ephemera. The official narrative, the CJ the family thought they knew, was so obviously false, a half-truth.

CJ was a brilliant storyteller. He would always put on voices when he told Joe bedtime stories, and Joe could still bring to mind the funereal voice CJ used when saying 'poor Mr Nibble' in the Blackberry Farm books. A brilliant mimic. So good at pretending to be somebody else. It felt like his childhood memories were being destroyed.

But perhaps CJ's transgressions, his other life, were his true shadow. He never seemed unhappy, so maybe that's just who he was, a man with two lives – CJ transformed into a stranger, inhabiting a place where memories aren't invited.

Up ahead, the train to Nottingham rattled over the railway bridge, unzipping the landscape, the light in the carriages flickering through the trees.

Rabbit. Where was she?

THE BATHROOM with its pod bath and porcelain tiles and enormous walk-in shower. The bedroom with its four-poster bed and decor in browns, deep reds and purples. Satin, silk, Egyptian cotton. Antiques. Random family portraits. Chocolates on the pillow. Baylis & Harding toiletries in the bathroom. Heavy dressing gowns. Tiny towels by the sink. It was the lushest hotel room she had ever been in.

Opening the window, she heard the bleats of sheep but nothing else – no cars, no children, no human sound of any kind. Canadian geese glided on the lake below, a lake edged with enormous chestnut trees and a solitary weeping willow, its branches teasing the water's surface. Across the lawn, the fields rolled up the mountainside, the top of which was cloud-covered.

She ran herself a bubble bath. Afterwards, she climbed into bed, listening. At some point, she fell asleep.

In the night, she heard a noise coming from either the corridor outside or the room next door. She blinked into the darkness, into the unfamiliar room. She checked the clock on her mobile, the dull light illuminating the worried look on her face. She sat up. Silence. She wouldn't let herself sleep again.

In the morning, she checked her phone. Fifty-three missed calls.

She phoned Cass.

'You have to tell me where you are,' Cass said, an edge of hysteria to her voice. 'The police think you're in danger.'

'Why, what did they say?'

'I had two detectives round here. They said it's a serious incident. They said they need to help you. They think I'm hiding something. They said I could be done for perverting the course of justice.'

'They said that?'

'There's a cop car parked outside. They're watching the house.'

'I'm sorry,' Rabbit said.

'I think you should come home, Rabbit. Running away won't solve owt.'

'It's all true,' Rabbit said, tears suddenly streaming down her face.

'I know, love. Just calm down. Where are you?'

'I can't tell you.'

'Please, Rabbit.'

'No, Cass. I'm safe, OK. I'm in a hotel.'

'You haven't done anything wrong.'

Rabbit sighed. 'I don't think people will see it like that.'

'Stuff people,' Cass said. 'Just get yourself back here. Please. The longer you stay away, the worse it looks.'

'I have to go.'

'Really?'

'Yeah.'

'Wait, let me get a pen. Let me write down the address. Just in case.'

That afternoon, she stepped out onto the balcony. The sky was deepening into night but there was still enough light to see the cars in the hotel car park over to her left. The wind tousled her hair and chucked her blouse collar under her chin. She palmed her hair back from her face and squinted at a car at the very back of the car park. The silver Mercedes.

She fell to the floor and crawled back to the bed, chastising herself for not leaving that afternoon. But she was just so exhausted, and felt safe there, in that old hotel in the middle of the mountains.

The room's telephone rang, making her jump. She listened, expecting it to stop. Maybe it was Cass. Maybe something had happened. She dashed across the room and lifted the receiver.

'Hello.'

'You have a visitor here in reception.'

'Who?'

'A Mr Frankie.'

Rabbit replaced the receiver, telling herself to remain calm.

It was possible to see directly into the reception area from the long, wood-panelled hallway. She would have time to hide if she needed. Cass must have blabbed. Footsteps in the corridor. A knock. Frankie grinned at her through the spyhole. She opened the door and jostled him in.

'How did you get here?' she asked.

'I borrowed a car.'

'No need to ask who told you. Did you see anyone following you?'

'No. Why?'

'You sure you didn't see a silver car following you?'

He shrugged. 'Loads. Why?'

She took his hand, led him to the balcony, and pointed towards the Mercedes.

'At the back, next to the hedge. You didn't see that car following you?'

'Why you whispering?'

'I'm not,' she said.

'Why don't you just ask at reception?'

'What?'

'If they know whose car it is?'

'You think they'll know?'

'The porter asked me if I wanted my car parking when I drove up. They probably know which car belongs to which room.'

'OK. Stay here.'

'What's going on?'

'Just stay here. And don't answer the door to anyone.'

Back down in reception, the receptionist smiled at Rabbit icily.

'Could you let me know whose Mercedes that is outside, please?' Rabbit asked.

'The Mercedes? I'm afraid not, madam. We can't give out information about other guests. Could you tell me why?'

Behind the receptionist, a porter stood in his shiny black

waistcoat and green trousers, hands behind his back and a stupid grin across his acne-covered face. The telephone rang. The receptionist glanced at Rabbit, and answered it.

'Thanks for nowt,' Rabbit said.

Rabbit scanned the room as Frankie talked, her eyes fixing on the poker in the old-fashioned fireplace. Brass, with a bulbous handle, it had a hook near the end for raking coals, like a giant fish hook.

'Look, don't blame Kate,' she said.

'You've got to be fucking kidding me.'

She rubbed her face. 'Don't give me a fucking hard time. My head's done in with it all.'

'What do you mean?'

'Will you stop asking so many questions?'

'Sorry.' He took a deep breath, exhaled. 'Frankie says relax.' She smiled.

A knock on the door startled them both. Rabbit dashed to the fireplace and picked up the heavy poker.

'Room service.' A man's voice.

Rabbit and Frankie stared at each other.

'It's the porter,' the voice said from behind the door. 'I've information about the car.'

Frankie opened the door a fraction. Rabbit stood behind him, wielding the poker.

'The car isn't registered to any room,' the porter said, 'but it has just left.'

'If you see it again, will you call?' Rabbit asked.

'My shift ends at ten, but I'll leave a note for the night porter. If you need any further information, I suggest you ask a porter, not the receptionist.'

'Right. Thanks.'

The porter stood there, smiling.

Rabbit sighed and said to Frankie, 'Give him a couple of quid, will you?'

Frankie tipped the porter and then climbed on the bed next to her.

'Talk,' he said.

2 A.M. RABBIT lies in the darkness, listening to Frankie breathing. Beneath the covers, she grips the poker, warm from her body heat.

A noise outside. A car, travelling slowly.

Leaning on one elbow, she peers through the darkness towards the window. After a couple of minutes, she lies back down. The panic rises. 'Relax,' she mutters. She stretches her legs, yawns.

Another noise. Tyres on gravel. The thunk of a car door closing.

From below she can hear voices, a low murmur. Footsteps in the hallway. Squinting through the darkness, she prods Frankie in the ribs.

He gasps. 'What?'

'Shh.' She points.

They both stare towards the door.

'This is fucking ridiculous,' Frankie says, kicking off the covers. He walks over to the door, and pulls it open.

'No one there, see?' He slams it shut and gets back into bed. 'Now, can we try and get some bloody sleep?'

The balcony door swings open, slowly. Rabbit gasps.

Night air fills the room. The curtains billow, the skin on her arms pimples. She turns on the lamp and tries to climb out of bed but her legs tangle in the sheets. The muzzle of a pistol slides between the curtains, glinting in the lamplight.

Frankie scrambles out of bed as a man steps into the room.

Grogan is tall, stocky, with a pulverised face. The Glock looks heavy, menacing. He takes another step towards them.

'Don't move.'

Rabbit's eyes meet Grogan's, a chill running through her body.

Grogan's eyes comb the room for a second before he levels the Glock at Frankie. 'Sit the fuck down, lad.' That thick Yorkshire accent again. 'Make a noise and I'll shoot.'

Frankie sits beside Rabbit, a protective arm across her chest. Frankie turns to look at her, eyes black holes, and Rabbit fills her lungs, about to release a scream, when Grogan aims his pistol at her head.

'Don't.'

Her eyes focus on the end of the barrel. A full stop.

I'm going to die, she thinks. This is it.

Frankie says, 'What the fuck do you want?'

Grogan drags a chair into the centre of the room and sits. He clears his throat. 'You thought I wouldn't find you?'

'I haven't said owt, have I? I've not been to the police,' Rabbit says. 'I won't tell anyone. I promise.'

Grogan shakes his head, tutting.

'You can trust me,' Rabbit says. 'I won't—'

A sadistic leer spreads across Grogan's face, eyes shining

with intent. 'I'm going to kill you and your boyfriend here.'

'He's not my boyfriend. He's got nowt to do with it. You can do anything you want to me. Anything. Just let him go.'

'Shh.' He waves the Glock in Frankie's direction. 'I'm going to make you watch.' He reaches into his jacket and throws something at Frankie's feet.

'Tie her wrists behind her back.'

'Fuck you,' Frankie snarls.

Grogan gets up from his chair, extends his pistol-hand, and rests the muzzle against Frankie's temple. Everything in the room concentrates on that trigger. Grogan then punches Frankie squarely in the nose. Rabbit recoils at the force of it.

Grogan puts his face into Frankie's. A single drop of blood hangs from Frankie's nose.

'Fuck you,' Frankie repeats.

Rabbit slowly leans back, reaching across the bed, until she feels the metal in her hands.

'Repeat that,' Grogan spits in Frankie's face. 'I dare you . . .'

Rabbit whips her right arm around. Feels the fleshy crack as the poker connects with the back of Grogan's head. He falls on top of Frankie, and for a second the three of them are a tangle of limbs on the bed, Frankie's and Grogan's fists a blur. The Glock goes off. A dull sound. Tissue. Cartilage. Bone. Mattress. Frankie doubles up, mouth opening and closing like a hinge with no sound.

Grogan falls off the side of the bed. Rabbit follows him over the edge. Hand sweaty around the handle, she brings the poker down onto his face repeatedly, the rake-hook creating deep lesions in his brow, cheek, neck. She feels his fingers digging into her legs. She strikes his pistol-arm and feels something give. Blood-filled eyes rolling in his head, Grogan swings the barrel wildly across the room.

Rabbit is blinded by the second bullet's flare.

Week Seven

A KALEIDOSCOPE of images shifted and overlapped in her mind. She felt like she was falling from a ledge, sinking and swaying as above her the surface, some kind of canopy, rumpled like silk. She opened her mouth to speak, ellipses of bubbles rising from her lips, disappearing as they breached the surface. Rapidly it became cold and dark down there, a skitter of fish flashing their scales, illuminating old boats and bicycles and cars covered in the scabs of rust . . .

Opioid dreams. Slowly, she began to resurface. A hospital bed, a place of malevolent shuffles of feet and the crackle of police radios in the corridor outside. Illuminated by the wax and wane of sunlight coming through the curtains, she observed figures, as if from a great distance. Doctors, consultants, nurses, police officers. They're helping me, she kept telling herself, but mostly she asked them to leave her alone. Blinking at the strip light on the ceiling, and then at the IV bags hanging around her bed like uninvited guests. Cass was there on the edge of things, fretting, fussing. White coats speaking medicalese. Hushed tones.

She suddenly remembered the flash, the iron smell of

blood. Leaning over to pick up the pistol and noticing spots dripping onto the carpet. She pointed the pistol at the man's head, blue vapour drifting from the muzzle. Her finger itched the trigger.

She placed her hand on her chest and felt the faint flutter of her heartbeat, and then closed her eyes to make the memories go away.

'How's Frankie?' she asked, her voice hovering between fatigue and irritation.

'He's recovering.'

'I want to see him.'

The consultant scratched his neck. 'That's not possible right now.'

'You're not lying to me, are you? He's going to be OK?'

'He's had major surgery, but he's stable.'

'He tried to protect me.'

'You're both very brave.'

'I don't feel brave,' she said. 'I feel like a coward. Tell me . . .'

'The bullet fractured his hip and pelvis,' the consultant said, 'and we had to perform an emergency laparotomy for suspected visceral and vascular injuries.'

'In English?'

'He'll be in a cast for three months and may be in a wheelchair for some time.'

Her arm ached. The 9mm bullet created a relatively small wound channel in her deltoid, the flesh of her upper left arm, which was infected with cloth fibres. The bullet just missed something called the brachial artery, which would have been fatal, the consultant said. They were going to have to keep her in hospital to monitor her response for a few days, to make sure the repaired blood vessels weren't leaking at the sutures and the infection had healed. Eating well, peeing well, vitals stable – only then could she go home.

'Will I have a scar?' she asked.

'There will be some scarring, yes.'

'And the man?'

The doctor nodded. 'He's been moved to another hospital. He sustained head injuries, but nothing life-threatening.'

'I could've killed him,' she said. 'I could have taken another person's life.'

'You gave him a good thrashing, but he'll live.'

Once the consultant had gone, she switched the TV back on and surfed the news channels. Kate must have heard by now.

As soon as Joe saw the mountains of the Lake District – appearing distantly like giant, two-dimensional cut-outs in the morning pall – he considered turning the car round and driving home. He opened his side window to feel the raw air on his face.

The hospital was swarming with police. A plain-clothes officer stopped him as he walked into the entrance. No visitors, under any circumstances. He left his card, and a message for her.

He got back in his car and drove around for a few hours, sitting, waiting in a pub car park overlooking a wide, fast-flowing river. Dark began to settle. He wondered if he should book a room for the night.

Just after 6 p.m., he got the call.

HER LEFT arm was heavily bandaged and there was a drip in her right arm, making her look even more vulnerable. When she looked him in the eye, he knew who she was.

He recalled the day he'd seen her at the lake. Remembered thinking she looked underfed, underdressed. How she'd eyed him warily, and when she'd pulled on the kite, her top had inched up a little and he could see her white stomach. Face hardened into a pinpoint of concentration. Those eyes staring at him now.

'It was you. At the lake.'

She nodded.

'And you knew who I was, didn't you?'

She nodded again, raising a weary hand. 'I don't want to talk about that right now.'

The anxious frisson in the room tingled in his veins.

'Sorry,' he said.

'No,' she said. 'I'm sorry.'

They held each other's gaze.

'Thanks for seeing me,' he said.

'What do you want, Joe?'

Immediately they reached a hiatus. Joe's mouth moved

soundlessly. He rubbed his eyes and he could still see the glare from the flashguns. The press had gathered outside the main entrance to the hospital, and, foolishly, he decided to walk straight through the middle of them all, the black foam of their microphones like a sea of punctuation he had to articulate.

The ties at one side of Rabbit's gown were loose and Joe's eyes inadvertently focused on the plunge of cleavage they revealed. She folded her arms across her chest and he slid his gaze towards the dark window.

'Is your Aunt Cass here?' he asked.

She tutted. 'Yeah, she's hiding under the bed.' She lifted a remote; the TV came on. She muted the sound and stared at him.

'I brought you these,' he said, handing her a carrier bag. Inside were a couple of magazines and a box of Celebrations he'd bought at the hospital shop.

She placed the bag in her lap without looking inside.

'I'm so sorry, Rabbit. Sorry for what you saw. Sorry it led to all of this. None of us knew what my dad was involved in.'

'Do you mean that?'

'Yes.'

'Really?'

'I swear.'

'Well, it's Frankie you should be worried about. He won't be able to walk for months. He might never be the same again.'

'I'll help both of you out. In any way that I can,' he said. 'I'm so sorry about all of this. But I need to know exactly what you saw on New Year's Day.'

'Haven't the police told you?'

'I need to hear you say it.'

'If I tell you, then I want you to do something for me. A favour.'

'Anything. Just say.'

She shuffled around in the bed, making herself comfortable, and began.

FIVE DAYS later and Rabbit was bored stupid. The police were still stationed in the corridor outside, though the detective told her they thought the likelihood of reprisals was slim. They had raided nineteen homes and business premises over the past few days, mainly farms in remote areas of the Pennines, and in three days' time, the man – Grogan – would appear at the magistrates' court accused of murdering CJ, and attempting to murder Rabbit and Frankie. The news brought little comfort.

They said it would be another couple of days until she could go home. Further observation, they said. Cass wouldn't leave her bedside.

'Is it me, or is it stuffy in here?' Rabbit asked.

Cass opened the window and Rabbit could smell the warmth of the day outside.

'I hate to say this,' Rabbit said, 'but you were right.'

Cass smiled. 'I'm always right. What about?'

'Sending Frankie.'

'I'd never have forgiven myself if anything had happened to you. Or him.'

'It *did* happen to him.'

'He's tough. He'll pull through.'

'I love you, you know.'

'Nurse,' Cass shouted, 'more morphine, please.'

Rabbit twinged. 'Don't make me laugh, it hurts. I dread to think what Frankie's mum's saying.'

'Don't you go worrying yourself over her,' Cass said. 'She says owt about you and she'll have me to contend with.'

Just then, a porter entered the room pushing a large chair on wheels.

Cass wiped a tear from her face. 'Come on,' she said. 'A certain somebody's expecting us.'

Rabbit administered a sloppy wet kiss to the top of his greasy head, stroked his hair, and kissed him again. Because he always wore a baseball cap, she'd not noticed before how his hair was thinning. Pale, waxen, he peered at her through a thick haze of painkillers, smelling of pharmacopoeia and sleep.

'You saved my life,' she said. 'I'll never forget it. You took a bullet for me.' She couldn't stop kissing him.

He cleared his throat. 'I woke up and saw flowers and thought I'd died.'

'You silly sod.'

'But then I thought it must be a mistake because I've gone to heaven.'

The three of them laughed. 'You will now.'

'Will you get off me?' he said. 'I might pass out.'

Rabbit and Cass sat on the chairs either side of the bed, eyeing the intricate system of pulleys and levers around him.

Frankie offered each of them a clammy hand to hold. He licked his lips and swallowed drily. 'Thanks.'

'Do you want some water?' Cass asked.

'I can't. They need to measure what's going in and what's coming out.'

Rabbit and Cass shared looks and then Rabbit started to cry again.

'I'm OK,' Frankie told her. 'Honest. I can't feel owt.'

Rabbit leaned over, kissed Frankie one more time, and said into his ear, 'I'll come and see you later tonight, yeah? When everyone's gone, OK?'

He winked at her.

ON THURSDAY that week, Joe, Eileen and Bill sat on the couch together, waiting for DI Slater to begin.

'We've been tracking a gang based around Sheffield for some time. We now believe CJ was working for them.'

Joe asked, 'Is this why he was in Sheffield that night?'

Before Slater could answer, Eileen asked, 'What do you mean "working for them"?'

'CJ was helping them with their financial deals. The gang have been cultivating cannabis at farms around the Pennines. They were also involved in money laundering, human trafficking and prostitution.'

Silence.

'Again, I must ask you not to say anything to anybody. We have to protect the integrity of what might be a trial by jury. The suspect is appearing at the magistrates' court tomorrow. Considering the amount of evidence against him, we strongly believe he'll plead guilty.'

Joe asked, 'So why were they chasing him that night?'

'The motive, we believe, was money. According to Grogan, CJ was planning to double-cross individuals investing in the cannabis farms – foreign investors. But that has to be verified. Rabbit, as a witness to the murder, just happened to be in the wrong place at the wrong time. At some point, the Crown Prosecution Service will issue a statement to the press that will reveal the full extent of CJ's involvement with the gang. I think you should be prepared.'

Later, sitting in his room, Joe wondered how CJ had met this new gang. Who approached whom? Had Lawrence set the whole thing up? And what were the new gang offering him? Enough to retire on? Joe wondered how the Stones would react when they found out the real reason CJ shut IFX down. That he was sick of Lawrence always reaping the benefits and had started working for a different gang, closer to home. Maybe they already knew. Maybe they thought Joe was involved and was privy to the paper trail that could put Lawrence away. Maybe that's why Lawrence had stopped phoning. Or had Lawrence been involved all along? Was Grogan lying?

He thought back to the day he searched CJ's computer and discovered that CJ had deleted a number of picture files three months before. Was he simply tidying up his hard drive, or did he have an inkling that he was in danger and was trying to hide things?

Joe tried to imagine what these images were.

In one image, he pictured CJ sitting with Beatriz on the yacht out at sea. He was wearing white slacks and a short-sleeved linen shirt. He was tanned, smiling, laughing maybe. The cat that got the cream. They were both sitting on the coachroof. Beatriz sat nearer the camera, but she was looking down, away from CJ and from the camera, with a bored expression on her face, as if she didn't appreciate what CJ was saying.

CJ had a spliff in his hand – some of Rose's home-grown – and he was talking about Eileen. No. The truth was probably a lot different. His family life was, perhaps, something they joked about. Derided. Snide.

The Mediterranean was so ridiculously blue in the imagined picture that it looked Photoshopped, and there was a man in the background, he was blurred but you could tell he was muscular – bald, bare-chested, and with a full beard. Lawrence. Neither Lawrence nor Beatriz had any idea what CJ had planned. Or had they?

That evening, Joe met Eileen carrying a bundle of Bill's clothes down the stairs. She assessed him for a moment before smiling, as if she didn't know how to react, and then said, 'Give me a hand with this lot, will you? Bill's been struggling with the stairs. It's best we move him down here.'

He took the clothes off her and followed her into the front room. What little furniture there was had been pushed against one wall, leaving enough space for a bed, wardrobe, bedside table and a rug. He tried to engage her in conversation but she gave him a frosty look and said she needed to make a few phone calls.

Once he'd finished lugging furniture up and down the stairs, and transforming the front room into a bedroom for Bill, he went looking for Eileen.

It was warm in the kitchen and smelled of fried onions and herbs. Eileen was staring into a cupboard. Joe walked over to her.

'You OK?'

She shrugged.

Joe kissed her cheek and took a seat at the breakfast bar. She closed the cupboard door, walked over to the sink, and began to attack some carrots, the click of the peeler filling the silence.

'You fancy some dinner?' she asked. 'I'm making shepherd's pie.'

'Yes. Thanks.'

'Set the table then.'

Let's act like nothing's happened.

He took the cutlery through to the dining room where the window was open and the breeze that came in was soft and smelled of Jawbone. Spring was almost here, electricity filling the sky above the valley with yellow light.

'There were all of these things going on inside your father's head that I never knew, and now I can't understand.'

Joe nodded at the wine bottle. 'Can I have some?'

'Off the wagon, are we?'

He poured himself a glass and held the wine in his mouth for a moment before swallowing.

Eileen's eyes filled with tears. Joe moved over to her.

'Come here.' He held her in his arms and squeezed her tight. He kissed her forehead, inhaling the comforting smell of her scalp, wanting to stay in that moment forever. He sat back down.

'We still haven't spoken about what's happened,' Joe said.

'What's to talk about? He's broken my heart and ruined my life.'

'If none of this had happened,' Joe said, 'he could've

263

retired in a couple of years and none of us would be any the wiser.'

'Thanks for stating the bloody obvious.'

'I mean . . . at least we know now.'

'And that's meant to make it easier?'

'No.'

'Once everything is sorted with the coroner, the death certificate and that, I'm putting this place on the market.'

Joe glared at her. 'You can't.'

'Don't go getting all sentimental on me, Joe. Do you not think I deserve a fresh start? Away from this valley? Away from everything that's happened.'

'But where do you want to go to?'

'I haven't decided. And you know all that money your dad filtered into our joint account?'

'The four hundred grand?'

'I'm going to give it to charity,' she said. 'A drugs charity.'

'All of it?'

'Every penny. I want none of it.'

'. . . yes. You're right,' he said. 'It's the right thing to do.'

He realised he wouldn't have a home any more. Homeless, fatherless. No constant, no safe place to return to. Take me with you, he wanted to say.

He reached across the table, took her hand.

'There's something I need to tell you,' he said.

'About what?'

He inhaled. Hesitated. 'About Spain . . .'

SIX DAYS after the shooting, the consultant said she could go home.

She visited Frankie before she left the hospital and gave him a big hug with her good arm.

'Thanks,' he said. 'I needed that.'

He chewed on a knuckle, pink-eyed from the painkillers. His storky, tattooed limbs looked out of place on the crisp white sheets.

'It feels wrong, leaving you here.'

'Look, I told you. Don't feel bad. About anything.'

'Don't say that. You almost died.'

'Don't matter. Seeing you leaving here, in one piece, that's enough. And knowing that bastard's behind bars. I hope his fucking head hurts.'

'Have they said when they're transferring you to Derby Royal?'

'They're not sure. It could be another month yet.'

'I'll phone you every day.'

'You better.'

'And I'll try and get up to see you as often as I can. I

265

won't be able to drive for a while.' She gestured at her arm and looked at Cass.

Cass said, 'We'll get you a lift sorted, I'm sure.'

'I'll be fine,' Frankie said. 'Don't fret.'

'Well, let me know if you need anything. Anything at all.'

'You know what I could murder?'

Rabbit laughed. 'I can guess.'

'There's a stash under my bed at home. If my brother hasn't smoked it yet. Next time you come . . .'

'I'll see what I can do. Give me another squeeze before I go.'

IT TOOK her by surprise. The first thing that hit her as she walked through the front door was the smell of flowers. Their mixed, heady scent lent the house a dreamlike quality. And cards. Over a hundred messages of support.

Cass saw her reaction. 'I wouldn't be surprised if every bugger on the estate was round here over the past few days.'

Rabbit touched the petals on a bouquet of roses and lilies. She read a few of the cards and her eyes began to fill with tears. The last time she was in this house, she was running away.

'Everyone's been so nice,' she said.

'I've only got one vase,' Cass said. 'I've had to leave most of them in the bath overnight.'

'Do you mind if I go have a kip?'

'Course not, duck.'

Rabbit headed up to her room. Cass had cleaned, and there were two framed pictures on the wall, the hand- and footprints she took after he died.

She stared at his tiny hands reaching out to her through time, waving goodbye.

His footsteps, walking away.

She got into bed and buried her face in the laundered sheets. In the fading afternoon light, she wept into her pillow until she fell asleep.

Week Eight

A WEEK later, she got a call from Joe, saying that he'd like to visit.

'What for?'

'Don't know. Just a chat.'

She said OK, but wasn't so sure. Everyone knew what CJ had been involved in, and gossip had it that the family knew more than they were letting on. Cass said they were bad news, the lot of them.

He came round later that day and they chatted in the living room while Cass pretended to be busy in the kitchen.

The woody smell of his aftershave filled the room. The mild-mannered way in which he spoke – he seemed so comfortable, so relaxed in his own skin, if a little distant.

He said, 'You know the favour you asked?'

She nodded. 'Yeah?'

'Well, one of the estate agents thinks they know of the ideal place, but it won't be free for another couple of months yet. It's a new estate on the other side of town. Dimple Bottom. Near the supermarket. It's nice.'

Rabbit laughed. 'Frankie'll love the name, if nowt else.'

Joe hesitated, and then said, 'I can help you out, if you want?' He said it without inflection.

'With the house? No, don't worry. I'm sure we can borrow the money. Besides, I've got some savings to fall back on.'

'I want to. It's only right.'

She sniffed.

'You miss him, don't you?' he asked, his denim-blue eyes watching her.

She swallowed. 'I hate the idea of him up there on his own. His mother couldn't give a toss. But I can't drive with this bloody arm.'

'Can't Cass take you?'

'She can't drive.'

'Well, let me take you, then.'

She frowned. 'Really?'

'Yeah.'

'When?'

'Whenever. Now if you want.'

She smiled a toothy smile. 'Really?'

'Yep.'

She checked the time on the wall clock. 'Can we make a stop at his mum's first?'

'Sure.'

'Don't say owt to him, mind, about Dimple Bottom. I want it to be a surprise.'

Storm clouds built the further north they drove. They sat in silence for a long time listening to the radio, driving through a landscape of low hills. Rabbit felt at ease in his hushed presence. He appeared to be a solid man.

Straightforward. But the expensive interior of the car made her feel cheap. As did Joe's designer shirt, jeans and shoes. The musky scent of his aftershave. His masculine, stone-like self.

They stopped at a service station just north of Macclesfield. Joe bought sandwiches and drinks from the shop. As they rejoined the motorway, Rabbit said, 'Let me pay you for the petrol.'

'No. Don't worry about it.'

She sighed, took the receipt he had just deposited in a recess below the stereo and read it. She took £40 from her purse, rolled it up tightly, and slid the cash and receipt back into the recess.

'Thanks,' he said.

They sat in an awkward silence for a while, until Joe cleared his throat and said, 'My mum's furious at Kate's mum.'

'Why?'

'She thought they were friends. Janet was a real rock when Dad died. But it turned out she was nothing but an idle gossip.'

'Like mother like daughter.'

Joe nodded, his eyes flicking from the road ahead to the rear-view mirror.

'You must really hate me,' Rabbit said.

He glanced at her. 'Hate you? What for?'

'For knowing what happened and not saying owt.'

Joe shook his head, and after a moment, he said, 'Do you remember that day at the lake, when you were flying your kite?'

'Uh-huh.'

'I've been thinking about it a lot. How it must have affected you.'

Rabbit ran her hands over her hair, peering into a passing car. 'I don't know what to say.'

'As far as I can see,' Joe said, 'most people's lives are chaotic. But Dad's didn't appear like that. He had us all fooled.'

Rabbit stared at him as he drove.

'I feel like I've got blood on my hands,' he said.

Rabbit was silent for a few seconds, and then said quietly, 'It was nowt to do with you, Joe.'

'I knew him less than I did a year ago,' he said. 'But that doesn't stop me missing him. I just wish he was here so I could give him a last hug. Get him to tell us the truth.'

At that moment, she had the urge to reach over. Touch him.

The gravy smell of the corridors. Patients wandering about in slippers and pyjamas as if they were at home. That feeling in hospital that everything is on an endless loop.

Frankie was asleep with the TV turned low. Outside the window, a pebble-filled courtyard contained a rectangular pond where carp drifted in slow motion. Propped in one corner, a pair of crutches.

Rabbit sat on his bed, nudging him. 'Hey, sleepyhead.'

He blinked at her a few times and then beamed. He sat up, rubbed his face. 'Bloody hell,' he said. 'What you doing here?' They hugged.

Rabbit hooked a thumb over her shoulder. 'This is Joe.'

'CJ's son?'

'Yeah.'

Frankie studied him for a moment and then stuck out a hand. Joe stepped forward, clasped it, and returned to his spot by the door.

'I hope you don't mind me coming,' Joe said.

Frankie didn't respond.

Rabbit pointed at the crutches. 'You walking now?'

'A few steps. But I've got to build up my muscles before owt else. I'm well glad to be out of that other contraption. It was medieval.'

'So you're making progress?' Joe asked.

Frankie studied him one more time, and said flatly, 'Yeah.'

Rabbit looked over at Joe; he appeared uncomfortable.

'Let me leave you two in peace for a while,' Joe said. 'Can I get you anything from the canteen?'

'I'm fine thanks,' she said.

'A tea please. Three sugars.' Frankie smiled. 'And biscuits, if you can find them.'

Once Rabbit saw the door close, she reached into her handbag and pulled out the tin of weed.

'Fuck me,' Frankie said. 'It stinks.'

He squirrelled it away in the bedside cabinet.

'So what's the story with pretty boy?'

'Nowt. He just offered me a lift. He said he wants to talk to us.'

'What about?'

She shrugged. Frankie shifted in bed, and winced. Rabbit wanted to see his hip, to see the scars, the damage.

'So how they treating you? That young nurse still giving you bed baths?'

Frankie was all goofy smiles. 'Yeah, I can't complain, really.'

'So when's your next op, then?'

Sheepish, he cleared his throat. 'Tomorrow.'

'Jesus. Why didn't you say owt?'

'It's no biggie.'

'Of course it's a biggie.'

He reached over and held Rabbit's hand. 'Don't look like that. To be honest, I don't want anyone to be here when I come round. I can't even be arsed talking most of the time.'

'You don't have to be polite with me, babes. Look, I'll stay over. I'll book a hotel.'

'No,' he said. 'You won't.'

'Really?'

'Really. But thanks.'

'Is your mum coming?'

'No.'

A knock at the door. Joe appeared with a polystyrene cup and a plate of digestives.

'So, Joe,' Frankie said, 'what do you want to talk to us about?'

Joe sat down, rubbing his hands on his jeans. 'You won't remember, but I used to know your older brother. He got me into weights.'

'Not really. Sorry. Is that it?'

Joe shook his head. 'I don't know where to start . . .'

'The beginning's usually a good place.'

'Don't,' Rabbit said. 'Let him speak.'

'I want to pay your legal costs,' Joe said.

'What legal costs?'

Joe looked at them both in turn. 'I've spoken to a lawyer. She thinks you should go for civil action against Grogan, as well as putting in a claim to the compensation board.'

Rabbit squinted into his blue eyes, wondering if he was being sincere.

Frankie asked, 'How much we talking?'

'Enough to make sure you're both comfortable. Until you're on your feet again. The kind of care you need will be pricey. Private care. Adaptations. Physio. General living and that. I think it's only right. Considering.'

'Aye,' Frankie said. 'Considering.'

THE FOLLOWING afternoon, Rabbit walked up past the Social Club, took the short cut through the overgrown jitty and headed across the top towards Kate's house.

Hands on hips, she stood in the middle of the driveway. A face appeared in the living-room window. Hannah, pointing and waving, followed shortly by Kate, and then Janet. The three of them staring at Rabbit for a moment. Mouths moving. Pushing, pulling. Arguing.

The curtain call.

Kate stared at Rabbit and Rabbit stared back. The memory was there in Kate's eyes, the memory of everything that had happened between them. Rabbit felt her eyes filling with tears. She wanted to scream; she wanted to hold her one last time.

Kate placed her hand against the windowpane, opening her mouth to say something, when Janet pulled her from view. A last goodbye. Her hand's condensed, ghostly silhouette, fading on the glass.

She was walking for roughly an hour, uncertain where she was heading. She noticed the theatre of spring had emerged along the roadside, crocuses, daffodils, pansies. The sky would start receding now, stop being so close and heavy in the valley like a wet blanket thrown over everything. Those raw, sunless days were gone.

She loved the first weeks of spring and she could see them so clearly in her mind: swifts, swallows and martins up from Africa, black arrows darting around gable ends, dive-bombing insects skirling over Jawbone and shaking apple blossom from the trees. She loved the pink, frothy candles on the horse chestnuts. And the black doughnuts of silage bags scattered across the fells like clumsy punctuation. Evenings opening out. Drunk-looking calves amid a spray of buttercups. The clicking of electric fences. Soon the woods and parks would smell of leaves, blossom and bluebells, the valley wearing its Hawaiian shirt of spring-time colour. But the season was tinged with a feeling of remorse because Jasper was a springtime baby. Five weeks from now, Jasper would have been a year old. Taking his first steps. One anniversary she didn't want to think about.

She walked up the hillside towards Needle Trees. When she reached Stark Tor, she headed across fallow fields and a swatch of moor populated with the dumb statues of cattle that stared at her. She walked past drystone walls, trying to distract herself with calculations: the number of stones per square foot times the length of the wall and hours of back-breaking toil. She pictured a wife in a ramshackle cottage, sitting in dank, freezing darkness, listening to her sickly children, waiting for her husband to return from his day on the fells stacking stone.

She found herself dropping down by the river again, just below High Tor. The gritstone gorge always filled her with fear. When she was young, her mother told her that giants used to roam the Peaks and the tor was a giant's tooth, lodged in the ground after a fight to the death.

Why people felt the need to scale the diseased-looking crag face was beyond her.

An eerie light filled the gorge. Currents of damp air rising from the surrounding woodland brought with them the smell of pine and spruce, gorse and broom. The sound of the wind through the high trees became the sound of wind rushing the radio waves the night she phoned the police. That crackle of silence down the line. The words left unsaid.

She wondered if she should leave the valley. Make a fresh start somewhere. Take Frankie with her.

She followed the river home.

That Summer

THERE WAS a window of glorious sunshine that summer, two weeks of sun parenthesised between endless, dreary rain, and it was still warm in the evenings, even after dark.

Joe pulled up outside the semi-detached property.

'Very fancy,' Cass said, leaning between the seats.

Joe removed his seat belt and handed Rabbit the paperwork.

Rabbit flicked through the pages.

'The place is fully kitted out,' Joe explained. 'He won't have to worry about anything.'

'Thanks,' Rabbit said. 'I really appreciate it.'

Joe said, 'When does he get out of hospital?'

'Three weeks. He'll be an outpatient for a while. Physio and all that. I want everything to be perfect for him when he gets here.'

'What about the court case? Will you both have to go?'

Rabbit shook her head. 'No, thank God. I really don't want to see Grogan again. It'll go to Crown Court in a month or so, but they said we don't need to be there because he already pleaded guilty at the magistrates'. The police reckon he could get twenty-five years.'

Joe nodded towards the house. 'I wasn't sure about the rent. I can always help . . .'

'Don't,' Rabbit said, and then forced a smile. 'You've done enough already.'

Rabbit and Cass stood in Frankie's new house, peering down at Joe waiting in his Audi outside.

'So what do you think of him? Mr Fancy Pants.'

'He's all right,' Rabbit said. 'His heart's in the right place, I guess. It's not his fault.'

'Hmm.' Cass ran a finger along the windowsill and inspected it. 'You might as well move in here,' she said.

'You wouldn't mind?'

'I know you. You'll be here all the bloody time anyway. He'll need help. God knows his mother couldn't give a flying fuck. How's his what's-it-called? His PTS?'

'He's still being assessed. They've got him on cortisol. The shrink seems to think he's doing well, considering. He flinches a lot.'

Cass looked fretful. 'And you?'

Rabbit shrugged. 'You know me, tough as old boots. You won't miss me?'

'Miss cooking for you, cleaning up after you, washing your dirty knickers? Don't worry, I'll be down to check up on you.'

'Promise?'

'Get off me, you silly sod.'

Rabbit kissed Cass's cheek again, and Cass said, 'Ey, what we going to do about Socks?'

'You keep him. He'll only go AWOL down here. I think he's happy to be home.'

Two days later, the Arms family were in the back garden under the brightening sky. Joe was sitting on the veranda of the summer house, a ramshackle affair that looked like it might collapse at any given moment, and Eileen was crouched in the flower beds while Bill sat reading a Western in the shade of an apple tree.

Joe was scribbling down the final ideas for his memorial speech. He was struggling with it. CJ's death had been explained, but what about his life?

He'd jotted down a few memories of his father, but nothing felt appropriate. One of which was the memory of lying in bed as a boy and listening to music in the dark, looking over at his bedroom door and seeing a crack of light, a warm orange glow, knowing that CJ was home and feeling safe. Another was of sitting at the top of the stairs whenever they had a party, listening to the voices, arguments and singing. The smell of alcohol, the cigarette smoke rising up towards him, CJ's voice usually the loudest. Sometimes Joe would wait until everyone had left and CJ and Eileen had staggered up to their room and then he'd go downstairs to scan the post-party scene, the bottles and ashtrays and bits of food on plates, lamps still on, crisps trodden into the carpet. He'd sneak some alcohol and cigarettes back to his room, get drunk and pretend to smoke, wishing he were the same age as CJ. Wishing they were best mates.

He kept imagining CJ as a sixteen-year-old, him and George joined at the hip. The fight, the fall, the devastation. Feeling like he needed to escape the valley. Those first few lonely months in Hastings. Meeting Asmina and Sattar. The fight in the club. A stranger in a new town. Reinventing himself.

Tomorrow, Joe would stand up in church and proclaim the man they knew in the face of public humiliation. Tacit in this agreement, and this act of defiance, was the knowledge that only then could the three of them possibly move on.

Distantly, the sound of an ice-cream van playing a hurdy-gurdy version of 'Greensleeves'. The sound of the summer.

Eileen dashed into the house to answer the landline. She wasn't talking for very long before she reappeared, walking through the long grass towards him. She stood very close to him, peering up through the leaves at an orange butterfly flitting about, her hand shielding her eyes from the sunlight. She was breathing hard.

'Mum?'

'That was the lawyer,' she said flatly. 'They're issuing a death certificate.'

Joe stood up, touched her arm.

'The lawyer said she's sending it to the Land Registry

and to the bank, to get the assets transferred into my name. They're also releasing the life insurance.'

She folded her arms and said, 'I thought I'd feel something. I thought I'd feel different. But I don't feel a thing.'

THEY QUICKLY settled into a life living together. Long peaceful days of recuperation. Frankie refused to talk about that night. He was seeing a counsellor and reassured Rabbit that was enough. No need to circle around it; no need to pick at scabs. Some faraway day it will all be just a memory.

It was quiet in the sun-filled back garden. The patio area turned out to be something of a suntrap and Rabbit spent every available minute outside, her skin turning from pink to brown, apart from the nodules of scar on her arm that remained iridescent. She sat on a tartan blanket wearing denim shorts and a bikini top. Hidden behind her sunglasses, the heat made her eyeballs pulse. At the end of the garden, a ten-foot buddleia sprayed purple cones like fireworks in freeze-frame, cabbage whites flitting among the leaves.

She sat eating a peach, juice dribbling down her fingers. When she got to the stone she spat it into the long grass, alive with the specks of insects, and wiped her hands on the rug. Above her, bed sheets moved in a gentle breeze. That heavenly smell of sunshine in your bed.

Frankie wheeled himself down the ramp with his camera, iPod and battery-powered speakers on his lap.

'Sort this shit out, will you?'

She took the stereo equipment off him and set it up.

Frankie pulled his T-shirt up over his head. Tinny sounds filled the summer air. Frankie in his camouflage cargo shorts and flip-flops. He fiddled with his digital camera, making electronic beeps, before passing it to her.

'It's going to be a noisy summer with these little buggers running around,' he said.

Rabbit squinted at the display screen.

'Flick through,' he said. 'There's loads. That button there. I took them earlier this morning when you were asleep. I was well shocked.'

The screen showed images of a vixen with her cubs.

'I counted seven,' Frankie said.

Cubs nuzzling, playing beneath the hedgerow. One chewing on a shoe. One playing with a yellow dandelion.

'Frankie, these are ace. I never knew you were a photographer.'

'Cute little things, aren't they? They're still grey, mind. Notice how different they all are in size. The covert is probably in the neighbour's garden, but they choose to play out back here.'

'I thought you poacher-types hated foxes.'

'Far from it,' he said. 'Got total respect. Wicked hunters.'

She passed the camera back and after a moment, he said, 'I heard Kate's not at the factory any more. I'm surprised she hasn't been run out of town.'

'I don't want to talk about her. You going back?'

'Where?' he asked.

'The factory.'

He sighed. 'Don't know. They said there's a position open for me, but I'm not sure. I was fed up with the place anyway.'

'Me too. I told them to stick it.'

'Really?'

'Yeah. I hate being on benefits, but fuck them. Fuck ice cream.'

'Maybe this is a chance for a clean break. Do something different.'

'My sentiments exactly.'

They both turned to watch a couple of sparrows, brown balls of puffed-up feather, dusting themselves in a patch of soil beneath the hedge. Even though she knew Grogan was behind bars, she brought to mind the image of Frankie exchanging blows with him and cast an eye around the garden, expecting to find him standing there with that death-stare look in his eyes.

'I appreciate everything you've done for me,' Frankie said. 'But don't let me hold you back. If you want to leave, move somewhere else, just do it. I'll be fine.'

'Don't be stupid,' Rabbit said. 'I'll be here.'

'It's not going to be fun. The physio thinks I'll make a full recovery, but it's fucking hard work.'

'Stick at it.'

He tutted. 'Course I will. She's fit as fuck.'

They laughed.

THE WATERS around Joe are much calmer now. The boat rocks gently from side to side, but still he fears the depths below. He lets go of the gunwale, walks unsteadily across the deck and touches CJ on the shoulder. Beneath the fabric of CJ's shirt, Joe can feel sinew and bone, and the hair on CJ's head is a mangy patch of what looks like fur.

'You're dead,' Joe says.

The structure moves closer. He can make out the branches of a tree and he realises his hand hurts. His palm is bleeding. CJ is turning fish-like, ichthyic, his bones razor-sharp scales. He can now see that the structure ahead of him is that of a church with a steeple like a witch's hat. It's the church beneath the lake.

The boat grounds itself on a beach. CJ leaps over the gunwale and heads into the building without glancing back. Joe looks around for some kind of an explanation but the darkness offers only silence. He steps out of the boat, follows.

Inside, complete stillness. The walls and floor glimmer darkly.

'CJ?'

Time feels different in here, like being inside a broken clock. A spotlight comes on, aiming directly downwards, illuminating a figure sitting at a small round table. On the table sits an ashtray, cigar smoking. The spotlight is super-bright and the effect onstage striking. CJ stares at Joe.

'So now you know,' he says.

Joe woke with a start and scanned the room, expecting to find CJ sitting there. For a second, he saw CJ's body in the lake, skin flensed and stippled, gnawed by underwater creatures. He shook his head, trying to push the images from his mind. He could hear Eileen clattering about in the bathroom. He sat up in bed and rubbed his face, breathing hard.

He walked into the church. Darkness, and then candlelight, a dry-wood smell. Flowers in the font, tables laden with Bibles, his shoes tapping on the church floor, across slabs carved with names and dates in Gothic script, some with carvings of ancient knights, others with angels praying. He wandered between the lines of pews and large stone columns twisting upwards to the ceiling. It was an odd setting to remember a man who didn't believe in God, but Eileen had insisted.

An hour later, the church was packed, pews a-murmur with the voices of friends, neighbours and strangers alike. A hush fell. Heads turned. Rabbit, pushing Frankie down the aisle in his wheelchair.

Joe nodded at Rabbit. Rabbit smiled.

The red-faced minister climbed the pulpit steps. Mouth spittle-wet, neck tendons protruding, he welcomed the congregation and introduced the memorial service, starting with a prayer and then a hymn. As the hymn finished, Eileen winked at Joe, and Joe replaced the minister in the pulpit.

Standing above them, scanning their blank faces, he

caught Rabbit's eye as she peered up at him, impassively. He coughed into his fist, licked his lips.

'I can't believe I'm standing here in front of you all, describing what it was like to have the man we're all here to remember as my dad.

'A strong character, as many of you know.

'We all knew him as CJ. He was healthy, strong and happy, with a massive appetite for life. His strength was reflected in the quality of love and attention, which he showed to his nearest. Although he wasn't always present when I was growing up, I have never doubted his love and support for me. It is the greatest gift a child can wish for from a parent . . .'

For those in the congregation who knew Joe well, he sounded different. It wasn't just the way his voice was tight with nerves, it was the way he spoke in another voice.

After he'd finished the eulogy, he folded up the sheet of paper and slid it into his breast pocket, his footfalls echoing out into the silent nave. He retook his seat beside Eileen and Bill. Eileen, sitting between them both, reached out, took their hands in hers and squeezed them tight.

The minister read the commendation and farewell with haste, because there was no coffin to stand beside, no burial, no rite of committal at the graveside, no handfuls of earth. Just the blessing of a body lost in a vast expanse of water less than a mile from the church.

Afterwards, the congregation filtered out, walking back into town or heading to their cars.

Joe sat alone in the gloomy silence of the north transept, thinking about the words he didn't say.

RABBIT SAT in the car waiting for Cass. She looked up at her old window. Empty.

Cass got into the passenger seat and gave her a kiss on the cheek.

'Ey up, me duck. You look smart. CJ's memorial?'

'Yeah. Just dropped Frankie off.'

'So how was it?'

Rabbit started the car, pulled away.

'I don't know. Sad. Weird. Eileen couldn't stop crying. Joe gave a speech.'

'Oh yeah? What did he say?'

'I think he was really nervous. I never realised how hard this must be on him.'

Cass looked at her. 'You like him, don't you?'

'Not like that,' Rabbit said, a little bit too quickly.

She drove the back roads through Darley Dale, Rowsley, Baslow and Grindleford to Upper Burbage Bridge. That familiar route.

They left the car and followed the scar of a footway through the heather and bracken, the single track that led along to a large stone outcrop. The valley was so barren and open to the elements that apart from the larch plantation below, the only trees were denuded firs, canted by the winds, twisted like gnarled old fingers reaching for the sky. You could see the dung-coloured town of Hathersage from there, scattered across the hillside about a mile or so away.

A curlew launched itself out of the orange sedge grass beside them.

'Jesus,' Cass said, and they both laughed.

What little light there was fell in a thin wash, and as they gyred towards the summit a stout, buffeting wind swept through the valley. It was the kind of wind that distracted you, slapped you around the face and demanded attention. It was becoming difficult to walk but they soon found shelter beside a huge boulder.

The clouds sundered and sharp afternoon light flooded the valley, honeyed and rich. Rabbit shielded her eyes and scanned the landscape. Higger Tor, Fiddler's Elbow, the twin peaks of Lose Hill and Win Hill, and in the far west, towards Manchester, a rain curtain was passing over the high ridge of Mam Tor.

A gloomy silence fell. Rabbit took Cass's hand in hers, recalling the night drives to this place.

As if privy to Rabbit's thoughts, Cass said, 'You'll meet someone one day, you know. They'll make everything that's happened this past year seem like a distant memory.'

'I don't think I will, you know.'

'You will. I promise you. But you need to think about yourself now. You need to move on, Rabbit. Move on from everything. Be good to yourself. Go on holiday. Take Frankie if you must, though I could look after him if you need some time alone.'

Rabbit shrugged. 'I'm OK, actually.'

'You've got your whole future ahead of you.'

'I know, and it scares the shit out of me.'

Rabbit threaded her fingers into Cass's.

'Thank you,' Rabbit said.

'What for?'

'For being such a good mum.'

The two women stood beside each other, holding hands, staring out at the landscape. The lush peaks and valleys stained with memory, and regret.

THE DELUGE began the following week. It approached over the moors and valleys, swelling the riverbanks, filling back gardens and gutters, distant thunder booming around woodland, crags and tors. Slate Lick River swelled at its confluence and burst its banks, river water lapping at people's front doors. Thoughts turned to the rising levels of Jawbone Lake, of CJ's body being washed along the valley in the floodwaters, turning up in someone's back garden. The rain drummed, bounced, shattered, drowned. The brief summer was over for another year. The sky getting down on its hunkers, lowering itself into the valley, clouds topping the hills. Nights drawing in. Soon, the first frosts would arrive, burning off the grass and summer flora. That lonely feeling autumn brings.

The Anniversary

JOE DROVE up the hill, along the freshly ploughed roads, to see his old house, and that familiar journey always took him by the throat. Nothing had really changed since he'd been away, everything in its right place, every tree, building, vista, but there was a new family living inside, no doubt preparing for Christmas tomorrow. A family with their own problems, their own secrets.

He parked beside the gates, the windscreen wipers thumping out an intermittent beat as snow whipped around the car, fumes of sifted snow curdling the air. He could just make out the old oak tree he used to play in as a boy. He would climb the tree and scan the hills often lost in the weather, thinking about the life he would lead when he grew up, a life far away from this valley. Now that he was back here, he wondered if things would have been that much different if he'd stayed.

Before he went abroad, he headed down to London for the final meeting with the purchasing company. They agreed to do the deal over dinner and drinks at the Brewery, an arty-farty venue in the East End. Attending the meeting were the new company's CEO, CFO, chief product engineer, a senior partner from the bank, together with a bright but soulless junior and a couple of £500-an-hour lawyers thrown in. Joe's broker kicked off the presentations, talking about sales numbers, year-on-year growth, case studies, statistics and financial proposition. It reminded Joe of CJ discussing the international exchange rate mechanism, the FTSE, DAX and IBEX. A three-times-profit deal was agreed, though Joe's main bonus would come from share options, released over time. He wished CJ were there to see it happen.

He'd spent the last four months visiting places he'd always planned to see – Croatia, Montenegro, Bulgaria, Macedonia – and celebrated his thirty-sixth birthday on a beach in Turkey. He'd met plenty of fellow travellers and had some fun, but mainly he just felt lonely. He'd stood on the beach on his birthday night, staring at the dim line of the horizon, the heat of the day's sun trapped in the sand beneath his feet, and he thought about Jawbone Lake. That's why he hadn't travelled too far, just in case he got the call.

Jawbone. They've found him.

He didn't think he'd return to London, to E14 and his apartment at Chinnocks Wharf. He was going to rent it out for another year and see.

Maybe I'll stay here for a while, he thought to himself.

He put the car into gear and drove the familiar streets to Bill's place.

He sat at the small wooden table opposite Bill, thinking about Eileen, wondering what she was doing at that exact moment. Joe cleared the plates from the table and put them in the sink to soak. When he sat back down, Bill asked, 'So where've you been today?'

'Back to the old house.'

'Ah.'

'It feels weird, calling it that. You know?'

Bill nodded. 'I've been meaning to go back up to my old place.'

'I can drive you now, if you want.'

Bill shrugged. 'So you doing anything tonight? Going out?'

Joe shook his head. They still hadn't mentioned the anniversary.

'Carol might be popping round early tomorrow morning,' Bill said. 'So mind on.'

'Do I need to be out?'

Bill tutted. 'She's only doing a bit of cleaning, youth, that's all.'

Despite his protestations, Bill had taken a bit of a shine to Carol, one of his carers, a tall buxom woman with curly black hair like a crash helmet and a dainty rosebud mouth. He'd begun to dress up every day in a three-piece suit, trilby hat and jazzy tie.

Bill moved over towards the fridge, staggering a little. Joe raised a hand to help him but Bill batted him away.

Joe said, 'I'm thinking of going to see Rabbit tomorrow.'

'Rabbit,' Bill echoed. He stuck a finger into a hair-filled ear and had a good poke around.

Joe asked, 'Has everything been OK in the valley?'

'What do you mean?'

'Have people been OK with you?'

Bill raised an eyebrow. 'You know what folk are like in the valley. They never forgive and they always remember.'

'And that doesn't bother you?'

He laughed. 'My muckers know the truth, and that's all that matters. So thanks.'

'What for?'

Bill tapped the back of Joe's hand. 'For asking. For being a good lad.'

Shortly after Bill went to bed, Joe called his mother.

'It's bloody freezing up here. I'm surprised people are going out. You should see the lights in the Old Town.'

Since the house sale, she had been staying with an old school friend up in Edinburgh that she hadn't seen for years. She went up for a weekend and had been there ever since.

Joe said, 'I bet it's great.'

'I really love the Kindle, by the way. Now that I'm getting used to it. Sheila's going to get one too. She says you're welcome to come up and stay any time.'

'I might just do that.'

She lowered her voice. 'You should see the house, it's bloody enormous. There's plenty of space.'

'I'm glad you've got some company, Mum.'

'Ee, we don't half have a laugh. We spent the afternoon looking at the brochures for cruises again.'

Joe said, 'You do right,' but he felt such a comedown because he realised his mother was now part of a sorority. A sorority of widows. Money in the bank. Taste of adult freedom.

Tomorrow, he wanted to say. Let's talk about tomorrow.

She sighed heavily down the line.

'I see you've been teaching Grandad some of your crap jokes,' Joe said.

She laughed. 'Who's this Carol he keeps going on about?'

'It's his toy girl, I think.'

'Don't. That's disgusting. Is he there?'

'No. He's gone to bed.'

'I've been wanting to talk to you,' she said.

'What about?'

'I don't know. Everything.'

'Have you been drinking?'

'I might have had a sherry or two. Why?'

'Sorry.'

'I just want to say . . . that I love you, son, and that I'm proud of you. I'm sorry I don't say it very often.'

'I'm proud of you too.'

'I was a bit hard on you this year.'

'No, you weren't. It's fine.'

'We'll get over this, you know. One day. CJ, the things he was involved in. I hate him for what he did to us. I'll always hate him for that. But I'll never stop loving him.'

'I know, Mum.'

9 P.M. ON New Year's Eve, they were sitting watching TV, the sweet scent of marijuana in the air. They had plenty of red wine and weren't expecting any visitors. Rabbit's mind was variously on Frankie's happiness and attempting to force herself not to think about the significance of the date. Three hundred and sixty-five days ago, she was in the Crow with Frankie, not knowing her life was about to change forever. But no thoughts on the crash could be permitted any longer. That day had done enough damage. Just look at poor Frankie – though sitting there in his pyjamas, dressing gown and obligatory baseball cap, he did look a bit funny, she had to admit.

From tomorrow, she told herself, she had to move on.

She cast a sideways glance at him. 'Want a top-up?' she asked.

'Thanks.'

She poured some wine into his glass and then watched the lights on the Christmas tree reveal their patterns.

'I've been looking into courses on the Net,' she said.

He glanced at her. 'Oh aye?'

'Aye.'

'Why's that then?'

She shrugged one shoulder. 'I'm thinking of going to college. But I have to do something called an access course first. They start in a couple of weeks.'

'Why didn't you say owt?'

'I'm telling you now.'

He studied her.

'Don't worry,' she said, 'I won't be leaving.'

'Good for you. It's about time you did something with that brain of yours. Speaking of which,' he said, holding out his hand.

She took the spliff off him. 'You sure you don't want to go to the Crow?'

'Why? Do you?'

'No. But I don't mind if you want to.'

He shrugged.

'You'd be able to cope on your sticks, wouldn't you?'

'I'm not sure.'

As he shook his head, her phone beeped. A message from Joe.

Going to Jawbone tomorrow

Frankie looked at her. 'Who is it?'

She stared at the screen. 'Joe.'

'What's he want?'

She paused. 'Just to say a happy New Year.'

Frankie turned back to the TV. 'Let's hope it is.'

She thumbed a reply.

Pick me up on the way x

'Let's just stay in tonight,' she said.

Frankie nodded, smiled. 'Aye, duck.'

THAT NIGHT, snuggled beneath the covers of Bill's spare bed, MacBook on his lap, he watched the images of his younger self on the screen – his four-year-old face looming and retreating, to and fro on a swing, Eileen chasing him into the spangling waves, CJ standing over him as he made castles in the sand. He could almost feel the warmth in the slim shadows and dappled light of the waves, running in bare feet over wet sand. Wiping the air with a wave.

He reached out and touched his face on the screen, reaching back through time, but it already felt like such a long time ago now, when they were young, perfect and familiar, his father still alive.

HE PULLS the trigger and shoots the choppy lake, squinting one-eyed through the tiny viewfinder. The wrinkles of the clay-coloured water, flecked with light, are caught on the celluloid of the Super 8, as is the green moss on the rocks at the water's edge. The shadows of the opposite hillsides stain the water ink-black, and the wind off the lake tousles Rabbit's hair as she leans back, tugging at the kite.

She feels him watching her.

She flies the kite with such style and technique, she has it trained like a bird of prey. Joined by two strands of tense string, by the invisible tug and heft of the wind, something comes together within her. She watches the lake churning the water, churning the past, and thinks about Jasper down in Coldwater village, the clutch of buildings beneath the lake, playing with his ancestors on the village green, her mother keeping a watchful eye over him. She sees a future version of him as a wire-haired, scruffy schoolboy, crying on his first day at junior school, the kite some kind of interface with the afterworld, and at this moment she experiences something like rapture.

She peers over at Joe.

He pulls the trigger a few more times but the film has run out. He slides the camera back into its black faux-leather case and then glances over towards the bridge.

Lately, he has tried to imagine that CJ's final moments were outside the realm of pain, that he had been sunk in some kind of dream, endorphin ecstasy, slowest swoon. Colours so vivid in that floating world, unreal world. A final, dim spark flickering in his cortex before all shut down and became nothing but a line of thought, a burst of pure energy that had no full stop, a single tone that continues to hum through Joe. Through Rabbit.

In time, she will feel that tragedy has come to inform her life, and this in itself creates a bond with this man, and the events of 365 days ago come to her in a wave of inner, arithmetical colour, making her smile.

She unwinds the string from her mittens, freeing the kite, releasing it to the air. The wind carries it, carving asymmetrical messages in a kind of kite ballet, before it tumbles from the sky.

He watches the kite hit the surface of the lake. He walks over to her.

They stand side by side, staring out at the red kite bobbing on the surface, as if sitting on a layer of black silk, until it slowly disappears into the water.

She reaches over and takes his hand.

He feels her hand in his, and something inside him shimmers.

Soon, the temperature will drop, and the surface of the lake will crystallise and ice over, hermetically sealing the world below for another couple of months. But maybe a fisherman will venture out onto the ice one day and drill a hole, piercing the gloaming world beneath with a shaft of tubular light, illuminating the clutch of buildings below where CJ floats in slow mo, spreadeagled through the murk and silt.

An underwater astronaut, lost in time.

I WOULD like to acknowledge the generous support and encouragement of Chris Simms, Vanessa Sutton, Nathan North, Peter Wright, Retired Detective Constable Paul Kettlewell, Julie Barker, Dr Anna-lyse Rowe, Alistair Dale, Steve 'Speedy' Bradley, Chas Robinson, Vladimir Gelev, Richard Rigby, Jonas Larsen, Charles Lambert, Alexei Levene, Sarah Phillips, Jude Johnson, Dorraine Darden, Andy Beverage, Peter Broadbent, Fraser Hamilton, Tony Walker, Katy Shaw, Detective Inspector Gary Tomlinson, Richard Speakman, Julia Chisholm, Chris Crouch, Lynne McCafferty, Emma Lannie, Mark Anderson, Scott Pack, and most of all Lucy Luck, Jason Arthur and Tom Avery.